BLACK TREE

Deanna Skaggs

Black Tree

To Arizona,

the land that adopted me when I was just a child.

"For where your treasure is, there will your heart be also.

The light of the body is the eye: if therefore thine eye be

single, thy whole body shall be full of light."

Matt. 6: 21-22

I.I

I closed my eyes. Willingly, I let the sight before me fade. With a reddish tone, only the light moved through my shut eyelids. So I convinced myself that since red is a warm color, the light surrounding me must likewise be warm. I focused on that red light, allowing all my senses to grow from it. My mind expanded and fed to me a new image. The blur that I saw of black nothing, glowing in redness, shifted to a blue desert sky embracing a land of rough, unkempt hills. This was the land where I had lived before; this was where I wanted still to be. But now I was far away. This land that I held in my head was the land I had deserted, all for intangible plans that I would never succeed in fulfilling, plans that had made themselves look so simple. This was the land before failure.

In this place, this innocent place, growing on my eyelids, the world was alive. Grasses blew in a dry breeze; saguaros reached upward from the ground; prickly pears kept fruits and flowers among their needles. Shades of color melted from pale white and yellow to green, brown, bright orange, and deep red. The sky was no limit to the edges of the earth because beyond the horizon of each hill there grew yet another tableau of warmth. On and on went the color and the plants and the life, beauty held within eternity. Only the desolate could not see the life here. Everywhere, there was growth and endurance. The very spines on a cactus were declarations of survival, perfect points to catch the water whenever it came. Where others ran away, those who remained persisted, and the land became rich.

I had delighted in living here before, and I delighted in the entire vision of it now. I felt powerful here, held up by this land that was in my very bones. The heat ran upward and I watched it make its way across the ground; its blaze of color lit up the whole setting. It was a lovely place. I breathed inward, wanting to taste the air. It would be tinted with the baked aroma of the sweet desert's vegetation caught up in the burning sunlight. That draught, so full of wonder, was the life force once offered to me, and the idea of drinking from it once again was irresistible.

But I had made a mistake. I had torn apart the image, once so clear and real, now so distant. That desert was no longer my reality: even if my mind didn't accept this truth, my physical senses did. Deliberately breathing in and anticipating a scent that was not there had ripped my attention from the fantasy behind my eyelids. The image dissolved. The lids lifted. Pain shot from my shocked head down through my arms. My physical sight returned in the dream's absence, but my heart retreated: it did not want to see reality. My heart had gone away to follow my desert, or to mourn it in solitude. It seemed that the two were bound together and so I believed that I could not keep one without the other. If I could not go back to the desert, then neither could I have my heart again, and my plans did not include going anywhere. I felt lost, pinched and desolate, in my heart's absence. There was nothing here for me to look at, nothing for me to feel, and nothing by which to feel. Experience dissipated, and life hollowed.

My weak fantasy, however, had taught me something during the time that it had overtaken my sight. It had shown me that the act of believing creates an image infused with more reality than that produced by the eyes. The eyes do not pay attention to what the mind does not want to see. Consequently, the absence of one's heart, which holds the capacity for faith, shades the eyes and bereaves them of their true sight. My vision, broken as it had become, remained muddled, and I was not sure what I saw in this unfamiliar land I had come to live in; it was so far from home and from all that I had learned to esteem. Why could not all the earth look and act the same? Why did life have to mean so many things, and why did my decisions have to bring me here, here to the place I did not love?

I closed my eyes and watched my heart run away until I could no longer see it. Eternity faded from my sight and all beauty vanished. I didn't know where I was, or when I was, or why I was. If eternity went on forever, then this moment that I was in went nowhere. I panicked within the silence.

I.II

The air was heavy as Abigail opened her eyes to the night. All light from the sun was long gone, but its heat was not. It lingered about in the form of thick air that moved differently through the lungs; it was not like breathing in a solid substance and it did not drown like water, but this warm air did hold more tightly to her throat and beg her lungs to move more quickly. Such a feeling ought, perhaps, to have been uncomfortable, but Abigail was used to summer heat; it came every year, whether she welcomed it or tried to fight it, and complaining only made it worse. Even on the days when the heat was suffocating, she accepted it. Tonight was one of those days of extra warmth; the air pressed hard against everything it touched.

Completely unnecessary, then, as far as temperature went, was the blanket Abigail clutched above her while she tried to sleep. Sweat formed a pattern across her skin despite the thinness of the blanket, yet nothing would induce her to remove the veil of cotton. She needed it; she needed anything that might help soothe her right now. Even her arms Abigail kept hidden away: the touch of the fabric released a comforting influence on her mind that she needed tonight more than she wanted physical comfort. Freeing her arms would only make her feel exposed and unsafe. Yet even while clutching her blanket, shreds of worry still made their way into Abigail's head: she knew that the quiet stillness of the night, however peaceful, could only be temporary. Chaos was everywhere, and danger could be very near. That was horrifying. Abigail's thoughts, pounding through her like the desert atmosphere, refused silence. Sleep would not come.

Gazing above herself in an attempt to find a distraction, Abigail found the wide sky, shining in black and white. Both colors appeared in complete clarity; two opposites stood in perfect juxtaposition. The stars smiled in the sun's absence as their giant, glimmering swirls mingled brightness with the dark atmosphere; the white glitter frosted the black background in an effortless gesture of beauty. Everything had such texture and depth that Abigail felt as if she could put her hand up into the misty setting and blend the host of celestial lanterns into the dark mist. Neither side, neither dark nor light, would protest the mixture: they seemed entirely happy together already. Yet the force of her hand could never be enough to move either the stars or the dark sky from their places. They were both too adamant, they who lived so high up above in the clear sky. If only the sky were closer to the earth.

Abigail sighed and turned from her back onto her left shoulder, knowing that the earth could never be so peaceful as the heavens. Now those faraway skies seemed too happy. She didn't want to watch such peace anymore, not when it was so different from the chaos on earth. Seeing the contrast was too painful: if the sky could not let its quiet fall down to the land, then why did it taunt those down below? As Abigail moved to face the earth again, her gaze fell to a pair of hedgehogs growing together a few feet away. The two cactus plants, on earth though they were, grew in harmony with each other. They didn't try to stay apart or take the focus for only one instead of both. Given the similarity in their sizes, they had probably grown together since their first day; maybe that was the only reason that neither one stood out more than the other. Gazing on them for a lingering moment, Abigail brightened as a second thought came to her mind.

"They're made of stars."

She could see it so clearly now.

Leaning forward, Abigail put two fingers around one of the needles of another hedgehog that was more within her reach. This cactus was dying, melting away from the top of its small tube body. Its weakness made Abigail's attempt to pull off one of the stars easier. With just the slightest tug, the needle she had put her fingers around came apart from the plant, bringing with it a whole collection of spikes attached to a tiny, central, brown circle. All the spears pointing outward from this central point came together to create a star, so clearly. And everywhere the skin of the hedgehog was made up of the outstretched needles, the arms of dozens or maybe even hundreds of stars pressed right against one another. How had she never noticed this before? Abigail saw the earthen stars so clearly now that she couldn't imagine looking at the cactus without seeing their shapes.

Pulling at another needle, Abigail found that it came away, complete with the rest of its star, just as easily as the first one had. She tugged at the hedgehog's spikes again and again, just to make sure it was true. Everywhere she pulled, Abigail further revealed a bare tunnel where the cactus was beginning to decompose into powder. Already the plant looked like a seamless part of the land, less distinguishable than it had been while alive: though it still kept its narrow barrel shape, its color and texture were different. It looked more like dirt and wood than the rich, succulent plant it had once been. When the spiky stars were finished fading, the cactus would become one with the land; first it would turn into a flattened carcass of black and white color and then into a barely discernible lump on the ground, visible only to the keen eye.

Just as only a keen eye would reveal the dead cactus, also only a keen eye could find the stars on the living plants. But now, everywhere, they seemed so obvious to Abigail. She shifted her gaze to a prickly pear. There, on the smooth green pads that were so different from the short barrels of the hedgehogs, were the same stars. These stars stood alone, evenly spaced out on the green surface instead of directly against one another as they did on the hedgehog. Yet still both plants held the delicate and fierce stars that echoed the stars up in the sky. What beauty there was here on these strong plants, so much like the reflected light from above.

Still Abigail did not feel much encouraged. This beauty was just another aspect of nature, existing in the plants instead of the sky. Was there really such a difference between the two? The plants were on the earth, yes, but plans were not people. In mankind was where she could never find such kindness and harmony.

Never? The question came silently to her mind as an echoing reminder. Abigail could not say that there was no compassion at all in the human world, even if it too often seemed that conflict was the only thing left on the earth. The life she remained living today was proof on the contrary. Some people could live every action with their hearts, and without receiving such compassion and protection Abigail would not have survived. That much she could not deny, however much the chaos lasted and the harmony dissolved into rarity. Some people could make everything seem better just with the simplest and most momentary actions.

I.III

I remembered them standing up against the barrier, clinging to the metal to get a closer look despite the long drop that fell in front of them. These children of mine were curious and eager. I watched them closely, and as I watched them, I also let myself look around. Beyond the two small heads I could see the ruins of Sinagua homes built into the earth many generations ago. This place was called Montezuma Well, not to be confused with the nearby Montezuma Castle, though visitors often went to both on the same day. Although it had a mini museum, which the Well did not, the Castle covered a smaller area of space; the greater length of paths at the Well had always made it my preferred destination of the two. I liked the opportunity to spend more time leisurely walking about. After all, the ruins here were still remarkable to look upon and every bit as worthy of being called a castle.

Rather than viewing the structures from below, we looked down toward them. While we stood level with the main ground, below us was a large bowl of water placed within the earth; the sides of the bowl were tall and steep cliff sides. This was the well, and its depth was great. Perhaps it did maneuver some of the attention away from the castle-like ruins simply because of its size and its unexpected presence. The water within the well flowed naturally from an underground spring, and the fact that it sat within such a deep bowl made it more intriguing than any lake. It immediately dismissed any notions that there was no water in this land where prickly pears and mesquite trees grew instead of green grass; water was just not always where you expected it to be. The water here liked to keep the surface of the earth in awe of where it hid, just beyond sight until you were right above it. Either its hidden state was a display of power or a way of helping us to appreciate its presence.

Looking across the water's surface to the ruins of a miniature city, I had always tried to imagine the lives, so many lives, that had passed by here. How different had everything looked then? What were their days like, and how accurate was the information we had about them? I wondered by what method, for instance, the original people had gone in and out of their homes day after day. Standing in boxy layers, the rooms and walls of the dwelling were dug into the cliff side opposite to where we stood, across the empty space above the well. Even if I had a wooden ladder, tied in place from the ground down to the dwellings, I could not picture what it would be like to climb in. Would the ladder go down to the dirt floor, or would it end sooner, hanging above the ground? Would I have to climb against the cliff, using it for stability, or would the ladder run across the empty air in the alcove? All of this was without even considering the long fall down to the water that would result from a single misplaced foot.

It was not that I was pondering over fear at the idea of living in the place; rather, I was in awe of the people who had made this their home. Such strength and such care they must have had, regular people though they had been. Delicacy and concentration, along with planning, had helped them survive, and acceptance and appreciation had made their days full. There must have been so much beauty in their lives from living directly against the earth and so much that, from a modern standpoint, I could only try and imagine. Yet I had sometimes felt like them, when I had walked up the steps to my apartment or even the short doorstep to my first home and whenever I wandered in outdoor places, like here.

My children had been more interested in the well than in the ruins; I suppose they had been too young to care about building homes when there was so much world to explore. They peered at the water through the metal bars and pointed out ducks that swam on the green surface. Patches of brown grew on the edges of the well, with some of it coming into the middle; it made the place look even more lush, like something you would find in a garden. Something complex and treasured was what this place became in the viewer's vision. Contrasting with the green plants that grew on the bowl's walls were the occasional, lighter-colored prickly pear and the dry, white rocks, worn down to a slippery texture by many footsteps, on which we stood. At least, the rocks were mostly white; in some sections, especially on vertical surfaces, the stone was stained black. It was the look of age and many years passing in this single place. So many feet and so many eyes had been here before us.

Angling down toward the water was a staircase made of this pale stone; here I needed to be extra careful. Although the way was rocky and without railing, the children scattered down quickly to the small lookout space at the bottom, level with the water. The steps were uneven and turned so often that I used to worry that someday the children would trip and tumble into the pool, returning to the earth by way of the spring. If it could shoot out life, perhaps it could also take it back. Out of caution, I always tended to see less of the views from here than from above because I was so busy making sure that no one did fall. My eyes were busy with the two heads of brown hair, the small limbs climbing down the rocky steps, and the young voices in a pitch so singular to me that it was sight as much as sound. Nothing could happen to them; I would make sure of that, however closely I had to watch them. Steep and crooked steps and deep water aside, my children were safe with me. My task of watching was simpler on our way back up, when their small legs were too tired to ascend the tall steps at any more than the pace of a whisper. I was glad for their tiredness only because it kept them closer to me.

There was also a second path that sprung from the main one after the well fell behind, but I had almost never, when I was with my two children, taken this other path. It was shady and cool, flowing right beside the river, an especially welcoming place on warm days. Yet, like the walk down to the well, the river path was at the bottom of rocky steps. Though these were less in number than the steps to the well, they were possibly even steeper, and that was too much for small and tired children. I had only come here with them as very young children, usually on my days off when my husband was busy with work. Now, so many years later, I took both side paths: now I was alone and I did not get tired. At least, I did not tire physically.

The land above this low path was bright and open and almost like the peak of a hill because of how the land beside it sloped down toward either the well or the river. After standing on such yellow and white openness, always it seemed strange to descend into the darkened, moist river area. You would not find a cactus growing here, as you would up above; skinny plants with voluminous, bright green foliage took their place. Trees shaded both the path and the river, making the space secluded and quiet. A sign just past the steps warned passersby of poison ivy, but I always considered this to be a sneaky way of keeping people on the path. Indeed, a simple sign marking the trail's end several paces away had, apparently, not been enough to keep walkers from clambering over the long white tree that grew, half horizontally, where the paved stones ended. A gate was eventually constructed there that, I thought, would probably be much more successful than the ignorable sign. People never liked to obey orders, but most were conditioned to obey barriers: it took more trouble to get past fences, and tangible barriers implied tangible danger.

Of the same stone as the pavement was a raised structure that served as both wall and bench. When you reached the end of the path, a cliff of earth was on the left, the pale tree straight in front, and the short wall to the right. This wall overlooked the river, and it was here that the edge of the path fell closest to the water. That was probably why there was a protecting wall here and nowhere else. This was simply another barrier, disguised as a bench for contemplation, yet this space remained a tempting place to linger.

I would sit by myself here at the end to rest and stare into the black water. The trees reflected into its surface and I felt like I could melt right into their dark branches. Looking carefully, sometimes you could discern small fish already there in the shadows. Your eye would lock onto one, then lose it again, but then you would see, without trying to focus on anything, a whole swarm of them within the wavering reflections of white branches turned into black echoes of themselves. The water turned to air and the shadows into plants and the whole world reversed into an unknown image of what it wanted to be, of what it thought that it was, of what it could never become.

I watched, and I clung to the stone bench, and I connected my eyes to the river until my head swayed. The longer I stayed, the more difficult it became to look up from the shadows of fish swimming through trees; that sight became all that mattered, for the moment, at least. Always my depressed mind fell into the water, so easily. It could slip and fall and fade into the branches of the river and see nothing else, nor worry about anything else but the coolness of the water, flowing back and forth through the shadows. Heartache drifted away into a drowsy numbness that remembered nothing and also, because it could hold onto nothing that was good, felt nothing worth feeling. My mind could not sleep here for long before the waking of reality came upon me. The problem was, I was not sure that I wanted to wake up.

Could I wake up? Could I wake up to the reality of the trees in the sky and the fish in the water, or would I forever melt them together into a reverse image of reality? Would I sleep forever in this silent aloneness?

II.I

The Heart. The Home. How could I find such things in a realm of buildings and streets and lights? Especially if they were awkward lights set to make me forget the sun's pure visage. There was no trace here of what I had come to understand as comfort and warmth. Everything here was tired and without rest, made cold with its isolation. Nothing repeated the harmonious lines of my previous home, where nature and progress had been built into one. I didn't understand the rhythm of this place, or how anyone could really be comfortable here. I felt odd here.

Where you belong. They were words spoken time and again as a reminder to listen to one's inner self, not giving in to a lesser position or one that was not perfectly suited. Everyone has to do something unique, this promising advice had said. I shuddered out in ripples of betrayal. Such advice only made me feel worse when life did not unfold in the way that I wanted it to or when I was unhappy for any amount of time. I had carefully thought out my decision to come here and I knew all my reasons for coming, so that must have meant that I belonged here. But I did not feel like I belonged. In fact, I was confused about whether or not I even felt anything. Where was my heart? Where could it have gone without me? I had not even the luxury to say that it was lost, given up to other aims that I had chosen before it. It wasn't left behind me, standing a few paces apart. It was . . . gone away. I couldn't feel where it was anymore. I was empty.

My heart had chosen of its own accord to bid farewell to me forever, as far as I could tell. I had never asked it to leave; I never would have done that since I didn't even know how to live without it. But its loss had to mean that my new position in this place was not compatible with my heart, even if I had, in fact, never directly chosen to abandon it. I had simply tried to consider a greater number of factors. That was all. Yet my heart had grown frustrated and upset that, for once, I had decided not to pamper it and make all my choices only with its fullest and sole consent; then it had retreated away by its choice, not mine. The traitor. Didn't it know that I was trying to take the best path, the path that would make me alive, fulfilling duties and finding joy? I hadn't meant for my decision to throw my heart away.

But wasn't that decision the strong, rightful thing for me to do? To separate myself from my emotions and view the situation rationally? To then take action based on this logic? Any preference I had for living in one place versus another had seemed insignificant. Maybe I had been wrong—or at least missed some other bit of information. Now, living in the results of my choices, I saw that the scope of rationality has its boundaries; its territory ends before you even reach the realm of the heart. And the Heart cannot peacefully be ignored. Thought and emotion need to dwell in harmony if there is to be any peace of mind. If you forget to pay attention to one, then chaos will result from the loss. Following only the Heart is confusing, like a road covered in thick and vaporous fog or warm humidity. But rationality only is cold and dry, painful in its waking and haunting in its sleep.

Even now, I tried to reach out and say, Heart, come back home to me. I did not mean to send you away; I did not mean to offend. Please, come back . . . I cannot survive without you. But the Heart did not hear me. It ignored me and chose to forget me, and I did not know how to go after it. If I didn't know why it had left or where it had gone, then how could I bring it back? I felt alone here without it. And being along, it was as if my new position meant nothing.

So where did that leave me? What could even be the point in my presence, fraught with weakness, here in this place? Was there a point in having come if I could no longer feel the Life in my limbs? Was I set for failure now? If my Absent heart could no longer pulse the blood through my veins, how could I live? And what good could I do if I was like the Dead? All meaning faded away from my grasp, and all contexts became confused. Everything I had heard or learned before this falling confusion I either forgot or forsook. I was left with nothing that could help me, nothing that I could see. If I could see nothing, then surely there was nothing there.

I scurried lost in the dark.

II.II

It had been a complicated situation, Abigail remembered. They had come and she had had no time to react. They had come and no one had realized that she was the wrong person. They had come and there had been nothing anyone could do to help— except for him.

It had been all very sad. She had tried to hold her breath. She had tried to not draw attention. She had tried to do what would make things easier on them both.

In the mornings they had come, leaving the night for fear of the future. Fear became, not knowledge of horror, but terror for what might come with the rising of the sun. The once synonymous words grew into darkly distant definitions, and terror became ever so much worse than horror. Horror was knowing what there was to fear, while terror was not knowing. Horror could be overcome; terror could not be defeated so easily because it came anew each time. By constantly changing, it continued fearfully guessing and wondering, never setting into a single place. Terror was exhausting and maddening, draining away all strength and courage while imagination raced before even the worst of reality.

Even hope had difficulty overcoming terror. And hope had not been easy to form at all in this place. They had tried to take away even the sun with Their cruel pattern of feared mornings. The sun was all that was good; it was light and warmth and hope, standing in contrast to the cold and darkened night in the prison. And so They had tried to take over this last connection with goodness, to associate the sun with the beginning of a new day's pain. Each morning, the light of the sun was allowed into the building just so that they could see their fear more clearly, just so that They could have more control over them. A new dawn became a new sorrow.

Sorrow, while they were held there in captivity, had come to mean different things. Abigail had never known that one word could mean so much. It had grown into simple things like hunger and heat and into monstrous things like disillusionment and betrayal. Though these were all difficult to face, Abigail had tried to hold onto what little power she had left and not become the betrayer herself, giving up what few secrets she had. Still there were those few people, on the outside, who had not yet been caught or discovered, and Abigail hated to think that, through her words, she might cause them harm. Of all things, that she could not do, so long as she had any strength left. So Abigail had followed Grey's lead and not spoken when there was no need or when she was the only one who would suffer from her silence. Perhaps, she thought, the pain that They caused to her because of her silence would not be so great as the guilt she would feel if she needlessly initiated a betrayal. At least, that was the thought that she tried to look to for comfort.

Grey, however, had come into this situation differently than Abigail had and so his reactions were also sometimes different. Abigail was low and unimportant, in the political sense. Grey had come as a leader, and as a leader, he was a person who cared about the pain of others. They knew this and tried to use it against him; this was the reason why, though it was him they wanted, they still kept Abigail. So, for Grey, there came a point

when Their prying for facts became political and his need to
protect Abigail became personal. This role of protector Grey
refused to forsake, even at the expense of the political. If he could
prevent it, Grey would not allow pain to endure in front of him;
in here, the war was abstract and he and Abigail were real. What
was real mattered more to Grey than what he could no longer see:
he could not, after all, know whether or not the information They
gave him was still true. For all he knew, everything on the
outside could be different now. They might be lying, and
everyone left might have already escaped or been captured, out of
reach of nearly any betrayal he could succumb to. His
information might be old and if he gave it up, he didn't know for
sure that it would even affect the others anymore.

Hope had come sparingly to them in this place and they
were left with nothing but trailing thoughts without form. Abigail
had wanted each night to escape into the bright expanses of the
stars, but they were hidden from her and she was just repeating
herself in a crazed delirium with her endless longings. The stars
became intangible and the earth flowed onward without her on a

plain of transparency that beat within the hearts of all the stars in the sky and all the animals on the earth; hopefully, Abigail thought within a timeless whisper, the people could hear the song that they sang. If no one listened, however, then no one would hear. They had to want to hear the song for its melody to become tangible again.

"The heart hears what the mind decides to see." Abigail spoke to the darkness of her cell, and she pondered the union of the body and the mind, in perfect transparency. A perfect code of transparency beat within all hearts, if only everyone would listen. The clarity was all there, clouded by imperfection.

Abigail leaned against the stone wall to have the feeling of something, if not someone, nearby. Sometimes she and Grey were left together, and sometimes, like this night, they were kept apart. There was no pattern to this form of terror, the terror of aloneness. There was only randomness meant to cause more pain. And the endless circle of new hope leading to burnt hope and then back again did cause pain. Although Abigail had not known Grey very well before, it was comforting to not be alone in this dark torment; she was always glad to have him near, just to have someone there who cared, and so she also worried about if or for how long they would be kept away from each other.

Sleep spoke out sparingly. Tiredness, Abigail learned, did not mean that sleep would be easy, even for a long time after she escaped from Them. Closing her eyes within this prison of Theirs felt wrong and unsafe; her mind could hardly ever settle down enough from its worries for more than a short rest. So Abigail stayed awake in the darkness and thought of the stars that would shine out in the night sky beyond the thick walls even without her gaze. That was what was so wonderful, and so frustrating, about the stars: they shined whether or not anyone was looking at them. While it brought hope to know that the stars were still there, that hope was too near to fantasy while the stars were so far away from view. It seemed to Abigail that if only she could have one glimpse at the stars and their eternal brightness, to prove that they were real, she would find comfort. But during all the time that she was with Them she had received no such gift.

It had been quite impossible. They had threatened. They had shouted. They had done everything.

It had been atrocious; they had held their ground; she had been scared; he had kept her alive.

II.III

I remembered panting lightly when I went up the steps to my apartment back in my college days. Those were the days when cares and worries were such simple things, always so easily overcome. Sweat traced across my skin under the hundred-and-ten degree Tempe sunlight as I climbed. The stretch of these stairs in summer represented eternity: the white of my shirt blended with the white cement, entwining me in its plight beneath the sky, while the sun above illuminated all. Whoever had built these stairs had probably not been aware that climbing them in the afternoon was like ascending the sun's throne: it perched right above the top step, glaring as you toiled. The sun's brightness became everything. But once the moment was over, I always healed instantly. As I bounced off the final step, already my mind began to focus on the joys of air conditioning and a fresh shirt that waited behind my door a dozen steps away.

I stuck my key in the first lock and then the second before jerking the door open. The apartment wasn't very old, but some places showed more wear than others, the front door included. It always felt tight in the frame, as if it didn't quite fit anymore. Though the indoor air was far from frigid, the air conditioning inside was shocking as it abruptly cooled the sweat on my arms and eased the red out of my face. The body always needed a moment here to adjust to the temperature difference: deep summer was always a time of contrast between full heat outside and much cooler indoor weather. Although I never knew how people had managed to live here in the days before air conditioning, such quick temperature changes were a challenge in their own right. Stepping into the apartment, I set my keys on the shelf, left my bag at my desk, pulled on a sweat-free shirt, and then poured a glass of iced tea in the kitchen. That was always the beginning of my relaxation, a routine short and easy that still led to calm.

I sat on the living room floor with my glass, as I often did after coming home, and observed the room around me. The once foreign apartment still had the same creamy white paint from when I had moved in before my sophomore year of college, but the walls were now covered in my collection. That was enough— and plenty of—personalization. A couple of paintings and a few nineteenth-century magazine prints accented some of my own photographs; the photos were images of the surrounding area, of trees in all sorts of places I had visited, and of old buildings I had come across. Hardly any of the wall hangings were worth anything to anyone except for me: the monetary value didn't really matter to me if I found something I liked. Besides, my resources as a student had been much more limited than they were now: I really couldn't afford anything truly valuable or rare back then. Yet I had invested what I could into my walls, always imagining that I would choose wall art over furniture if I had to.

Nothing could compare with imagery, even if you had to sit on the floor while enjoying it.

I had not, however, made this compromise. I did have whatever sparse furniture I needed in the room; sitting on the floor right now was my choice, not a necessity. The living room held my desk and chair for schoolwork in addition to a small, leather sofa for when I felt like acting normal instead of sitting on the carpet. My plan was to wait until I had more space and a more permanent home—not to mention more income—before pulling my attention from the walls to the floor. Then I would be able to do more than nail up pictures, mere projections of my reality. Then I would finally create my reality, own every detail of my life. Slowly, the future would become tangible, starting with such material things as tables and chairs.

For this moment, however, I was here, making my way through graduate school. Every step of my journey took time. It seemed a long time had already passed since I had first come to this apartment, and perhaps it would yet be a while before I left. Even after I graduated once again, for the last time, there would be little reason to leave this apartment until I had saved enough money to move somewhere significantly different, unless, of course, I received a job opportunity elsewhere. But I wasn't counting on this last possibility: I was beginning to see myself remaining connected to this university, in one form or another. It wasn't that I wanted to ignore other potential situations and careers or that I didn't want to challenge myself by going somewhere different; I just thought that my contribution here could be equally important to what it could be anywhere else. And I liked it here. What was so very wrong with choosing and keeping what you liked?

I finished my iced tea.

Schoolwork kept me occupied for the rest of the day, leaving little more space for musing thoughts. At least, I could only muse on the topics I was studying; they were enough to fill my mind twice over and then some. My main task on this day was making my way through a pile of books for a research paper. The books that I had already looked at had colored paper sticking out at intervals, marking whatever passages I wanted to use; I had also made notes in a side notebook to describe why I had marked these particular sections. In addition to the time I needed to spend on the rest of the books was the constant reviewing of my notes as I reformed my thesis in response to new ideas. I never really knew, for certain, which book might have what I needed for my paper topic, so I made sure to go through plenty. And sometimes I would happen on a random fact or opinion that would call me into an entirely new direction, a new direction that meant more exploring.

By studying history, I had banished myself to valleys of pages. There was always much of reading, or skimming, or deciphering. But this was the subject that most intrigued me and made me feel most at home. I had always thought it would be worse to settle for a field of study that seemed easy; it wasn't always the workload, but my degree of interest in the work, that made a task harder or easier. Yet it was also because of my interest that I had so much work to do: I went deep into each topic, wanting to get the most out of the learning and studying.

It was true that I wasn't quite as miraculous a historian as were some of my peers. A couple of them were drawn to tactile history, antiques and artifacts and such; others could spend weeks wearing archival gloves and deciphering written documents. These students would be the ones to come up with the latest breakthroughs in the field of history. Everything was tangible to them, and they approached the field like science, something to be understood, interpreted, and added to with new findings. I wasn't really one of them. I was more about memorizing the various names, dates, and places associated with events or time periods and interpreting the conclusions that other historians had already drawn. I liked to visit physical places and learn about them, but then to bring my knowledge back to my desk. Perhaps that was why I was considering remaining at the university: that path seemed to suit me better. And being a professor offered its own opportunities; I could still, from this position, keep up with the field and pass on what I had learned.

So even if I had to live in a temporary home while studying my field, I deemed the compromise fair: I was on the path towards what I wanted. Life held all kinds of moments, and they did not all intersect all the time. This moment was about learning and waiting, planning for the future and looking forward to it without being jealous of it. My need for patience was no different from what nearly every other college student dealt with, slowly waiting for the years to go by. Time itself was temporary and did not last forever. Once this moment ended, it would never come again. If, in the present, I worked to achieve my goals, then I would be glad, in the future, that it was over and done and accomplished. In this way, every difficult situation came to have a purpose, provided I gave them all proper attention and focus.

And in this way, I had managed during my college days to hold the pieces together. The work and the waiting and everything else that I went through did not tear me apart because I knew, back then, what I was doing—and what was coming after. I had my future planned, and in that plan I felt safe.

I hadn't realized that plans are not in control of everything.

III.I

The glue that held my bones together had dissolved at some point, and I felt too weak to exert the necessary effort to hold myself together without it. I didn't even want to try: just the idea was too much, creating in me even more fear. I was not ready, no, not ready to be strong enough for such an exertion. Instead of fighting against the breaking bones, I crumpled down, forever bent by pain. So stilted, my posture fell even deeper and I didn't try to change. I thought I needed to be independent to stand up, so I stayed down because I didn't know where to find strength for independence. And I didn't know where it would be safe to place dependence, if there was any such place. How could one person stand independent of any other forces, and how could there be anything great enough to allow for dependence? Either way, independence or dependence, I thought all solutions for standing strongly were out of my reach.

That was how weakness worked. I understood that much. I understood that much even if understanding did not help me to escape. I could see the invasion of chaos in my head, growing against the walls and pillars of my mind and sending out vines of despair to my senses. The message the vines sent to me said that I was helpless. I had no evidence to use to argue against them, so I listened to what they said, and I couldn't imagine not listening to the hopeless signals. The tangled vines made me so confused and tired and the signals came so forcefully. I wandered through a tumultuous forest, slashing my arms this way and that and then giving in to the vines once again. There was nothing that I could do, no, nothing for me to do besides to give in.

My captors within weakness, they tied me down. They blinded me. They finished me. And I didn't fight them. I didn't even want to try. They took my will away from me, and my reason. I thought that to fight them, I would have to take my hands and detangle the knotted vines and find my way out myself, and I didn't even know where I would begin such a task. The vines of weakness were so many and so thick and I didn't understand them, even though I recognized their presence, so how could I unravel them? Maybe if I could just tear them apart like veins of blood vessels, it would be easier. I could cause pain, just not clarity. Yet these thick, growing vines that existed apart from the flesh were harder than mere bones and sinews to break; that was an easy task in comparison. My hands alone did not have the power to tear away such tangled vines.

So I lived through my crumpled life, feeling rather alone.

I could, it was true, walk straight and talk normally during the daylight hours, leaving no clue to outsiders that I was not whole. When it came to the outside world and what I let it see, there was nothing wrong, nothing at all: being compelled to put on a front, I succeeded in doing so just as well as did the next person. If none of us could tell what was beneath, then I had no reason to think that there was, after all, anything peaceful beneath anyone's guise. So I convinced myself that all the faces I saw were hiding their pain and their terror and their oncoming weakness just as I was. I wondered if we were all wearing fronts for different reasons or for the same reason. Maybe all of our individual reasons, spread so far apart, came back to the same combined root.

I wore my front every day, but regardless of its neutral façade, my mind was lost like an autumn leaf. First its life was pulled away as the cold winds blew it from its tree. Then it was crushed on the ground by someone's foot. I couldn't heal myself and I couldn't find my way back to the living tree from which I had once grown.

I was forever fallen, lost to the mystery that ignites life and to the harmony that unites it. Could crumpled leaves really live forever?

III.II

All from the cruelty of mankind was this living death. Because of the endurance of this evil, which was completely separate from care and peace, life had waned further away from their limbs with every setting of the sun. Inside this prison They had shown that life, physical life, is something tangible, and as such, it can be stolen away. Daily They had dangled it from their fingertips as if it were a toy, subject to any whim. They taunted them, showing that whatever else They could not touch, this They had control over. And all they had been able to do as Their prisoners was to watch the changing moods of their captors and to ache in their bodies as the pain began anew or strengthened to a climax. There was nothing else.

No one could keep a complete hold on sanity in this place, not all the time, at least. Sanity needed some measure of peace, and the mind could not keep up with all of the feelings and thoughts that came to it here. Abigail, however, tried most of the time to stay in command of her mind. That seemed like the right thing. But she didn't always want to try: it seemed easier not to try. And it didn't even feel right to fight back when it hurt so much to do so. There seemed also to be little point in remaining sane. If trying to stay sane only made everything hurt more, then keeping emotion locked in would only quicken the insanity she had tried to avoid; it was all a circle in her mind that left no escape from darkness. So Abigail sometimes let the insanity have its battles within her mind and did not try to stop it. Sometimes insanity, as confusing and misleading as it was, was easier to bear than straight pain.

I'm upset at everyone, Abigail had cried out within the circles of her mind. At you and at them and at me. No one is doing what they should. Why do you stiffen when I say should? What's wrong with that word? Should. I'll say it again. Should. You only don't like the word because you feel threatened by it, but I'm already threatened. I fear no words, least of all the word that I am on the right side of, unlike you. Ugh, I'm going crazy. You'll help me? Please do help me. I need help. I need a brink of sanity to hold onto. I need something to tell me that he cares, even if no one else does. Where is he? Where are you? Please, don't let go. I'll stay with you; only you stay with me, also. We need to stay together, even if it doesn't make sense. Even if we know nothing more. If I can just make this work, if we can just stay together, then maybe everything else will be set right, too.

The sun rose; They returned.

The sun set; They left. Darkness, even without Their dark presence, returned.

Help me, Abigail had cried. Don't you care enough to do that? How can you have forgotten everything? Aren't there some things that everyone knows? Who are you? Do you remember enough of life to know who I am? Who am I? I am the keeper of the terror of the night. I am the partaker of the horror of the day. And you, my friend, you are the Horror of the Day. You multiply the darkness and promote its power, you the Horror of the Day. Yes, that's you, dear. If only I could say it to your face. Then maybe you would remember. But you already know it, don't you? Yes, that's why you're here. Please, never let me be like you. Please. I'd rather be like him. But he's here, and I am here for trying to be like him. I have succeeded, and success is not sweet. If we were like you, we would not be here, unless we were on your side of the chains. But that would be worse, wouldn't it? To be like you. Do you know what tears are? I think you may have forgotten. They're what fall from my eyes onto your face, trying to make you understand. Please don't do this. Who are you? Why are you? Do you know? I know. I know and it hurts to know, for your sake. Maybe someday we'll both know. Maybe we'll both say it out loud. I think we will. I'm sure you don't

50

know now, otherwise you wouldn't be who you are. I mean, you wouldn't do as you do. Or you shouldn't do as you do if you only knew. How could you? Oh, never mind. The distinction doesn't matter so much right now. It's your choice. I've made mine. And I'm tired. I wish I could rest. But I can't. Not here. Perhaps never again.

The sun rose; They returned; the sun set; They left; Darkness resumed.

Darkness, Abigail had cried. Are you there? I'm here, waiting for you. Just come to me now and let it be over. I know you're there. I hear your voice speaking out like velvet. I hear your song like thunder across the surface of the earth. Why can't I see any lightning with it? Maybe some rain? Wait, what am I thinking? There are no windows here. I can't see lightning without windows. I can't see anything. Too bad. Lightning is amazing, a spectacle of awe in all of its sharp brilliance. Don't you think so, Darkness? But maybe you don't agree. Maybe you don't like lightning. Lightning would make you brighter, less dark. Maybe you wouldn't like that. Sorry, friend. But I could do with a little light sometimes, even if you're quite content without it. I mean, not like daylight. That just feels different now, tainted as if I can no longer enjoy it. Or maybe it isn't different. Maybe it's just that the daylight would feel better if I weren't here anymore, seeing it only through the veil of this place. But I think I'll always be here. Maybe I've always been here. He says that isn't true, that I used to have another life, but how can he be sure that I have ever been anywhere else but here? I mean, even he agrees that we haven't known each other for long. So how can he know anything about me? How can he know anything apart from who I am now, where I am now? His name is Grey. That's all I know.

Wait, that couldn't be right.

What had she just been thinking? Surely her mind was not so far gone already that she no longer knew who she was or how she had come here or who Grey was. Surely even the coming of insanity wouldn't obscure such simple facts. Abigail hadn't expected that: if she didn't, in those moments of pain, lament the loss of sanity, at least she lamented the loss of understanding.

The ability to understand was perhaps, after all, the core of sanity. Without understanding, everything that she stood for would be gone, lost and forgotten by the long hours of darkness. Could there be anything worse than forgetting why she had chosen to resist Them and what it was that she was holding onto here in this cell of black sorrow?

It was thus that, day after day, pain grew out of itself in layers to create this eternal moment of having no power. Abigail was so close to drowning in such a great wave of aloneness and powerlessness. There was nothing else, for one timeless moment of darkness.

III.III

I remembered settling into my car with my daughter to fall in behind the moving truck, which my husband was driving to our new house. His car was already there waiting for us. As I looked down the cement sidewalk of the familiar Scottsdale street for the last time, I considered the place where I stood. The ground here stretched level and flat; only the grassy area behind the sidewalk sloped slightly. The sun above shot down bolts of heat; similar waves moved off of the black parking lot. Everything moved in a patterned motion of planned reflections and reactions. That was the problem here: everything that the eye fell on was too synonymous. I needed the health of incongruence now rather than a bed of things built for comfort. The flaw of cities was that they tried too hard, and the pretense of perfection hurt too much. There was no real variety, only created variations: parks to break up the blocks of buildings and planters in the parking lots of shopping centers. Prescott would be better: it was big enough that I would not lack a movie theatre or choice of grocery stores, yet small enough that there I would be able to live. There I would be able to see forests of trees and hills of rock and less of cement and harsh lines.

"Fare thee well, Valley of the Sun," I announced to the view in the dashboard as I eased my car onto the road and prepared for a long and slow drive behind the truck. It was still early enough in the morning that Charlotte was already beginning to doze in the backseat, so she didn't answer anything in reply to my words, if she had even heard me. I drove from then on in silence, except for the quiet commentary of my thoughts within me. Despite the slower speed of the moving truck, traffic wasn't at all heavy that morning, and I soon found myself leaving the city limits. Here at the outskirts was where the alluring drive began, once the landscape was allowed to emerge.

The expanse of the sky shone as a pearly canvas of white, utterly bright and clear all around me; I pictured it as the daytime garment that the sun wore during its waking hours above the land. The sky's scope grew as the buildings faded, though my windows somewhat limited my view. Even from behind metal and glass, however, I could see and feel the sun's arms reaching out in welcome. Only the car's air conditioning kept the heat at bay. Though perhaps I left behind the Valley of the Sun and there would soon be a perceptible decrease in temperature, still would the sun itself be with me ahead. Even though I was moving to a different region, I was remaining in Arizona, and therefore not everything would be different.

Yet it was because of how much the landscape changed in the duration that the drive out of Phoenix had always fascinated me. It was a journey of living, developing beauty that fed no expectations. Though the city appeared to be roughly in the middle of Arizona, it was in fact in the southern half of the state, which was part of the Sonoran Desert. And the rest of the state, which was not part of the desert, included a great deal of diversity in its climates and landscapes. Driving even an hour or so away from the Phoenix area revealed a different type of land. The shape of the hills shifted from rocky here to peaked there or from cliffs to gentler plains, back and forth from one to another. The saguaros, which outsiders usually pictured growing everywhere in Arizona, gathered together to give you one last farewell until you turned a corner and found that they were gone entirely; they belonged only to the South. All at once, you drove upwards out of a rocky, desert area and found yourself in a clear field of land much flatter in comparison both to what came before and to what was coming after.

That moment felt as if you were ascending into a sacred land. It looked something like a prairie because of the grassy, yellow land and clear sky, yet there was more texture here. The plain grasses and wide sky were accompanied by a canyon splitting into the land to the right and a cliff edge falling downward to the left. That edge, in turn, led to a line of mountains with smaller foothills at their base; if the mountains had been a castle, then the cliff's deep fall could have been a giant moat. The mountains were tall and bulky, the main land flat and quiet, and the canyon open and inviting and rough and even green, depending on the season.

Sunset Point this place was called: if you came in the evening, the sun set directly into the mountains. What made the sight strange was that you could watch from the main piece of land and feel as if you were in a different world from the mountains. Though the mountains were not very far away, the drop of the cliff edge and the moat-like depths made the distance more powerful. Watching the mountains from here, you felt like you were in a high place far up in the sky and isolated from all worry. You could watch everything happen so far away and not need to react to any of it except to say that it was beautiful.

After passing Sunset Point, it became more apparent that the road moved north. Green bushes began to plant themselves across the land, quickly becoming more frequent. The vegetation all around grew more pine-like and the colors darker and more pronounced: the only kinds of cactus left were prickly pears, and even they were fewer here than they were farther south. During my time in the Phoenix area I had come to prefer the more traditional desert landscape of saguaros and creosotes, but pine did have a romantic look to it. Adventure stories might take place in the desert, but a cooler setting was more suited to the heart; and I was no longer looking for adventure. It was the calm and collected atmosphere of hard work and contented results that, coming into my early forties, I had sought. I had had enough adventures: they were always tiring without always ending well; there was no control over adventures.

Andrew my son I had lost already at this time; my daughter, just six years old, I hoped to raise in a more friendly world. It was the same world, I knew, but I imagined that the separate environment would make her safer, as if I had done something to keep her from sharing in Andrew's fate. I could do nothing more for him, but this much I could do for her. In any case, Prescott would be a good place for her to grow up in, as it had been for me. In Prescott she would have summer heat, falling leaves, and winter snow; every season ran its course here, and there was plenty of space to enjoy the outdoors at every time of year. When she was older, she could go to the movies or the mall with her friends, just like she would have done in Phoenix, and then come home to her family afterwards. She would be happy and safe here. Since I planned to continue teaching, my commute would be long, but I wasn't the only professor who had chosen to live outside of the city. If others could handle a long commute, then so could I. With my husband transferring to a position in Prescott, at least one of us would always be close by if Charlotte needed us for any reason. In this way, the change in cities would work out for us as a family.

So it was that, on a strong summer morning, Nathan and I had moved to a three-story Victorian home on the tree-shaded street of S. Mount Vernon. This street of historical houses was where I had always hoped one day to live, and finding one of my favorites for sale just when we were ready to buy one made me infinitely happy. I adored the house; I adored the layout; I adored everything about it. Living room, dining room, and kitchen were on the first floor; there was a library on the second floor; the third floor held the master bedroom. I didn't mind having so many stairs because I couldn't imagine this home without them, as a single level house. The stairs made the house tall and elegant from the outside and made the rooms, on the inside, small and warm. There was a balance between grand and cozy; the beautiful and the livable were one.

We had painted the exterior in shades of green before moving in, so the house appeared fresh and new even with all of the historical value. Inside, some of the walls had stenciling to mimic the patterns of Victorian wallpaper; the floors were wooden and the furnishings already mine. I had filled the house with my old tufted leather sofa, my books, my pictures, my mahogany dining set, and my remaining family. Our previous home had been much smaller, so Nathan had helped me choose whatever additional items we now needed. The library, with its built-in shelves, was our favorite room; we chose two leather armchairs to keep there. Nathan's vintage maps were on the walls, and our new rugs softened the wooden floors. We bought a smaller table to keep in the kitchen and a gold mirror for the foyer. This green Victorian was my dream home and very nearly my dream life, built with Nathan at my side. We decided that, in this house, we would be able to heal and to continue our lives together in happiness once more. The future would be brighter after such darkness.

That was eight years before it happened and I became alone again. So much for memories.

IV.I

I accidentally spilled some water one day. I envied that water. It was able to do what I could not.

Most of the water I was able to wipe off of the wooden floor right away with my sleeve so that the wood wouldn't be ruined, but there were still traces of its dampness left. I hurried away to find a dry cloth to clean the rest of it; when I returned with the cloth, however, all the dampness was gone. The water had left no trace of itself. For all my fears about not being able to clean it quick enough, I couldn't tell that it had ever been here. There was no sticky residue, no faint bit of color, and no more wetness on the bare wood. What virtue did water hold that it could react in this way? Tea or wine would have left a mark. Or what was so special about the air that it could lift up and dry the water so easily, keeping it off of the open floor?

I was not like this water, so in control and so ready to begin anew. I had spilled out onto a new environment, and I sat there still, confused and vulnerable. Had I really chosen on my own to come here? I certainly didn't act like it. I felt like I had been banished here, as if this were the very edge of the world and it had nothing to do with me. Instead of reaching out to find the friendliness here so that I could settle in and build my life, I waited hopelessly for a dry cloth to help me up and take me away. I began to think that I might wait a very long time, an eternal waiting with no end, unless I could find some way to adapt. I did not understand this environment, its people, or its land, but I would have to understand it in order to live here.

Otherwise I knew I would have to leave.

Much as I complained, I didn't want to give in; I did react, however weakly, to this knowledge of what I needed to do. This was why I tried to spend time each day outdoors, walking even if I had nowhere to go and whether or not I always enjoyed being outside. I was trying to become familiar with this place and the definitions of its components; if I spent time in the deepest and worst part of this land, which was by the water, then maybe I could make it mine. But day after day, this change refused to happen. This place continued to feel entirely foreign to me, as if I could never be part of it.

It seemed always that I walked across water, without course or purpose. My feet slid from the path and my eyes couldn't see through the fog. It was not that it was horribly humid here, nor constantly raining. But compared with what I was used to, there was water everywhere, in the air and in the ground and in my line of sight. Did this place wish to drown me? We all needed water to live, but this was too much; I was not a worshipper of water that I could form every part of my day and of my life around its presence, swimming within its grasp. And yet there were times when I was completely surrounded, when I saw and felt nothing but the water that set out to engulf me. I didn't know what the purpose could be in so much wetness. If my head were dunked beneath water, all that would happen to me would be a loss of breath. I needed breaths of air more than burial by water; I needed life more than death, and how could water offer me this?

The water that I had spilled in my house dried easily enough, so why did all the water beyond my household borders remain so constant? It was like the liquid was alive, presenting itself everywhere, and I tried to face it, but it felt so strange to walk through waves. The water shouted at me, but I couldn't understand any words. The world turned wet and cold, and my skin wrinkled and my bones shivered. Perhaps I had never been designed to live in a land of water. Perhaps someday I would float away, uprooted by the moisture and my own confusion.

IV.II

And she had watched him never waver. After all the threats, an ultimate day had come. They had asked Grey to tell the impossible, the information that could put so many people at risk, only to keep her safe. His words would take everything away from the resistance inside the city. Didn't They know, with all of their calculated threats, that she was the wrong person? It wasn't her They had meant to take; she wasn't Grey's love. It was Alice; it was Alice for whom Grey would give up all. Not Abigail; Abigail meant nothing to him personally. Yet Grey did stand up for Abigail, all the same, in the end. He gave Them the information, and he saved Abigail's life. That was more kindness, compassion, and heart than all the patterns the stars made in all the sky.

And Abigail had watched him give what he had worked so hard for simply in order to protect her from Them. Part of Abigail was relieved, only she did also regret what this would mean for those on the outside of the prison. If there were any of their number left in the city, they would all have to flee now, if they could: all of their security was now gone, and it hadn't been much to begin with. Hopefully they would make it out of the city to the group of survivors, the same group that Alice and Grey had planned to bring Abigail to when they left together. It was Alice who had first told Abigail about the group, about how they lived together for protection but were also forced to travel constantly throughout the desert. Because they were always on the move, it was difficult for Them and their sparse team of scouts to find the group, although friends and other fugitives always managed to track the survivors using hidden means. At least that still remained a secret: if They ever learned how to track the survivors, there could be no more resistance and all would be over.

Yet They already seemed to think that nearly all was over for those who stood in resistance. Abigail worried sometimes that they were right, but Grey assured her that this was not the case. He said that even the information he had given up would not make the difference between endurance and failure. It would feel like things were over for those who needed to flee, but there were other plans at work, he said. On the whole there was hope; there would always be hope. And that was the second gift Grey gave to Abigail: the gift of hope. He had saved her life from Them by giving up something precious, and then he had made that life worth saving by instilling her eyes with light. Although they were in darkness again that night, they had been allowed to stay together this time. And so they had talked through the darkness.

"Do you think they will get out of the city safely?" Abigail could only picture how badly her own escape had gone. And that was when they had thought they were acting on advance notice. No one would be able to give the rest of them advance notice.

"Hopefully most of them have left already, when we were captured. They would have assumed that I would not be able to protect them anymore. And they would have been right. I have no power here, not in that way. Those who stayed in the city would at least have known the risk of choosing to stay."

"Thank you, Grey, for protecting me."

"I know that we're nearly strangers. We barely even knew each other outside of here, and we still barely do, even after so much time in here. The only thing I really know about you, Abigail, is your name. But I also know that you are one of us. And that is enough. Just that tells me so much. Anyone who has chosen to not follow Them is worth protecting. We give each other hope in this way, just by knowing that we are of the same mind and choice." He paused for just a moment. "Don't ever let the darkness swallow you, Abigail."

"I do always wish the darkness were over, and yet I also dread the sunrise. Tonight, though, it seems alright. This moment is bearable, and I feel little of fear or worry. I can't see anything in here, not even you so close by, but it's as if I can feel the moonlight around me, outside of these stone walls." She pressed her fingers against the raw stone as she spoke. "You know how it is, when the whiteness lights up all the silhouettes of everything, almost as clear as daylight. It's soft and sharp at the same time. Everything becomes new under the moonlight, and somehow seeing the familiar world in this new way makes you breathe and think more clearly."

"That's called peace." Grey's voice was quiet now, hushed into a roughness barely above a whisper as though he was no longer talking out loud. "That's what it's called when the world is still and quiet and simple. When fear is cast away into the shadows where it belongs, and beauty is the only thing that comes into view. The truth comes into clarity, and it is beautiful, and it is all you want to pursue. When everything feels in its proper place, or at least nothing feels as if it is in the wrong place. That's when calmness comes."

"Yes, maybe that's it." Abigail sighed, lamenting that the view of moonlight was still nothing but a dream and yet managing to wrap herself within that dream. "Peace, no matter what is happening. Everything is still the same, but your vision changes. Because as afraid as I have been here, I almost feel better now. I feel like it doesn't matter as much what happens next: I have already faced fear and death. If, next time They come, there is nothing to save me and my life ends, that will be that. I only hope for the chance to see the night without bars once again before that happens. I miss the moonlight. Whatever the resolution inside my mind may be, pain still exists, and that's hard. I'm in a daze right now and I can't feel it all, but I know pain will return and make me tired and aching. So I admit that it would be nice to leave this place, even if only for a moment. I want to see the full world around me again."

"I couldn't agree more, but, Abigail, we must not talk about that any longer." Grey's voice sounded serious and urgent, setting an end to their talk of dreams built of moonlight.

"Very well. I just wanted to say my thanks to you once again. I won't forget."

"I was glad to help you, glad to make any difference here in this place. The chance to lessen the harm They do does not always come, and it would have been a great harm to lose you."

Such a simple and yet costly rescue as Grey had given her wasn't an act that Abigail could ever return, yet she didn't feel worthless or in debt. She felt thankful: the only way to repay an act of kindness was by creating more kindness. Otherwise Abigail would take away the very reason that Grey had pronounced her worth saving.

IV.III

As it happened, I left the university not long before the accident. The decision to leave had made sense to me: I had enjoyed university life as a student and as a professor, but my time there felt like it had reached its conclusion. I had felt something new coming, and I had thought to prepare for a slower pace. Leaving behind the long commute, which had begun to wear me down, would give me more time to spend with my family. The beginning of Charlotte's high school years had reminded me that I only had her living with me for so much longer; I had planned to make the most of that time. Yet I had never wholly abandoned a career outside of the home: instead of classrooms and an office, my new domain was a shop on Antique Row. It was both a laid-back enterprise, in comparison to the hectic schedule of the one I had left, and an occupation still based on my longtime interest in the historical. Everything about my choice had seemed right.

When the accident happened, the changes shifted: all of the constant factors were what I had lost and everything new was all I had left. I wondered if I had been banished here all alone.

Yet whenever I looked around, even with my sense of loss I could not help but remember why I had chosen this new path for my work life.

Like my Victorian house, this shop had been part of my mind's consciousness long before it ever became my own. Coming here every day felt right; this at least was a place where I belonged. To welcome in passersby, a window display covered the front of the shop, with a double-door in the middle. The counter with the cash register was on the left as you walked in, standing parallel to the left wall. When I stood behind the counter, I could look out both to the window on my right and to the store within. This way I could keep an eye on the people coming in and out and on those who were inside. There were, of course, still areas of the shop, behind the shelves and half walls separating the different booths, that I could not see. But overall everything was close within my view. The large room was shaped like a rectangle with the street side being one of the shorter ends; an open, upstairs area stood in the back section of the building. The staircase to this floor was also on the left side;

wooden railing followed the steps upward and lined the edge of the little room, creating a balcony effect. Because it was more difficult to bring large pieces up and down the stairs, there were only a few of them leaning against the walls upstairs; otherwise, it was mostly smaller items there.

Antique stores, I thought, were always best when they felt, in a certain way, like houses. That made customers comfortable and products easy to find. The store, like a home, should not be dirty or messy; I wasn't running an indoor yard sale. The selection of products, as well as their placement, must be tasteful. Often, the vendor system enhanced this overall look: the different booths became like the individual rooms of a house, each with something different to offer. One vendor would sell books to create a library; another would focus on kitchen items. There would be the frilly section with hats and gloves and the tougher section with rusty tools and vintage machinery. When everything was put together correctly, it always felt welcoming to come into such a shop. If not, then no one would want to buy anything or even come back a second time. Further, if all of the items were arranged well, different types of people would feel comfortable finding their favorite booths or quickly focusing on the jewelry or vintage toys or furniture or whatever they were after.

Despite the fact that my books and other possessions had always been in my office on campus, this shop, filled with things that were not really mine and never would be, already felt more like home than the office had. The office had been for work and for research, my students' or mine. The store was for pleasure, my customers' and mine. I had enjoyed my work at the university, but it had come with a certain kind of formality. Here there were rules and routines to keep to, but everything else felt more casual. I had come here anticipating peace and a new stage in my life, one apart from expectations. But why did the peace of this place have to be tested so soon? I had barely had a chance to enjoy less time spent driving, less emphasis on dates and deadlines, and more time with family before, against my will, it all changed again and everything I had just chosen took on a different meaning. There was no Nathan to share my beautiful home with and no Charlotte to create a safe and comforting life for.

Of course I went back to work soon after it was over. What would I have gained by staying away? Nothing would make me feel better, and I couldn't abandon a new business: although the shop had been an antique store before, it had never been my antique store. I did not do everything the same way as the previous owner had, and any business needed a leader, anyway. My shop assistant couldn't do all the work for me. And, in any case, I no longer had any reason to stay home. I had started working here in Prescott so that I could spend more time at home, but now my motive for being at home was gone, buried beneath a speeding car. Maybe speed had always been my doom, waiting to steal from me, and that was why I was drawn to quiet.

I glanced out of the glass windows. Today's weather had been gorgeous, mild and temperate, probably a prerequisite to a rainy evening, so I had propped a door open to let the place air out. An old building plus old items did mean that there was more dust in the air, and stuffy air did not help with ambience. Yet it was only so often that the door could be open; though often pleasant, the weather was not perfect at all times of the day or year. So I took advantage of those few moments of clear and still weather, even if they didn't last a whole morning or afternoon.

While I watched the clouds gather outside with the approach of evening, it began to rain, just as the calm daytime weather had suggested. A few drops touched the sidewalk, then more followed. The light gray grew dark under the invading water. Only slightly flustered, I rushed over to close the door: no one would thank me to chance getting any water inside, whether on the shelves or the floor. But I wasn't thinking negative thoughts about this turn of the weather. Though it was the sun, not the clouds, that I loved, a late summer storm was a thing of beauty, an outpouring of the sky's soul. Rain was what connected us to that blue dome above. The clouds stayed up in their heights, whereas the rain came down to meet us. And that was very exciting.

Rain also meant a change of pacing for the store. Those who were already inside took their time lingering over every shelf: they were reluctant to leave and risk a drenching. Usually a couple of passersby flowed into the door, seeking a dry spot to wait out the heaviest part of the rain. These people were generally of two types. They either felt obligated to look around and find something to buy or they saw no point in pretending that they wanted anything more than to get out of the rain. And, indeed, this latter group was right, in a way: even customers who had planned to come in didn't always buy anything. Antiquing was about the searching, not always the finding, and sometimes the searching took time. Still, it was my duty to wonder why anyone would not want to browse my store with great interest.

Today's rain was typical of the season. It quickly built up to a torrent, loud and forceful and intimidating. Like someone had dragged a knife through the belly of the clouds, water poured onto the sidewalk and street. Such rain always felt, for a moment, like it would never end, or would at least continue for hours on a time. It wasn't always like that, though. Certainly there were days when the rain didn't cease until it had drenched the land and turned it into a giant puddle. But there were also days like this, when the rain came out with such vehemence that it grew bored and decided to stop just as quickly. Or maybe the clouds were bored to begin with, and finding too much water within their grasp, had tried to be rid of it as quickly as possible. Maybe they just didn't want the bother of a slow drizzle.

However the rain's end happened, my temporary customers were glad that they would be able to leave without a long wait and without getting soaked. I watched them end their brief foray into my territory, wondering if any would return on purpose. Sometimes different worlds met like this without result, but sometimes such meetings stirred up new interest: a potential customer might be anywhere and any of them, previously uninterested in antiques, might suddenly realize that there were things here which interested them. Or maybe they did enjoy antique stores but had never found their way into mine. There were many possible stories, and I always liked to run them through my mind. I did hope, however, that these thoughts of mine did not mean I was looking too closely for friends and family in casual customers, that I was really so hollow inside that

I had nowhere else to turn. Store relationships were just fine and this was a social place to be, but I would still have nothing to do at the end of the day except to return to my empty home where there was nothing but aloneness. And that had never been my plan.

V.I

I was beginning to have trouble seeing the benefits of my choices. By now they should have been blooming and ripening like white blossoms and sweet apples on a branch, but I saw nothing of the kind. I knew why. I knew that I could see no fruit forming because my eyes were clouded over in discontent and worry that prevented them from seeing anything positive. And, conversely, there were no fruits to see, anyway, because my eyes were sitting too much in that storm. Nothing looked as good as the way that I had thought it would all be, months ago when I had planned to come here, and that bothered me. But this was not the way to create results, by holding onto everything I did or didn't do and wishing it were better, or at least different somehow. If I did not believe in my cause and focus on bringing it forward, then it would truly fail.

I didn't want to fail. I didn't want to give in. I wanted to live my life as happily and successfully as anyone else. But each time I woke up, the morning felt heavy. The air weighed me down against the bed, and then the cloudy sky seemed to push me deeper into the house instead of letting me leave. It was as if I fought them daily in a personal battle against nature, though nature had once been my friend. And the battle wore me out so much that, during the day, I didn't care as deeply about what I was doing. Focus was difficult among all this distraction. I let opportunities drift by with the clouds, and I carried my limbs around instead of working out potential freely. I felt as if I wasn't really needed here, as if I was achieving very little. At least, because success was not forming in the way or the shape that I had pictured, I thought that it wasn't forming at all. Success didn't blossom gigantically in front of me, and so I thought that I had made the wrong choice to come here.

Success, I was beginning to see, is not accidental. It does not simply happen without reason or form, and it does not quickly or easily happen, if it happens at all. Success takes devotion.

But then, as I began to make this realization, I wondered what success was, after all. People spoke of it in so many contexts that what did it really mean? Was it solely monetary, solely spiritual, solely familial? Social or ethical or personal? What was it really, and was there only one way to find it? Was it a single moment, or did it include the whole journey towards itself? If it was a journey, then did you have success only at journey's end; was everything leading up to it empty time, or was it also some form of success? No wonder I wasn't succeeding if I didn't even know what success meant, if I was barely beginning to think about what it might mean or could mean and yet was still obsessed with obtaining it. I had once pictured that the world was a much more simple place with definitions that came instantly and effects that came clearly.

I realized that, while certain ends were achievable without wholly believing in a cause, the ultimate result would be hollow as a tree trunk. I had observed this much at least in other people. The bark would appear sturdy and strong, while the wood inside decayed without a life of its own. Solid success, the best kind of all and the only kind worth working toward, needed a base and it needed belief and devotion. The base, I decided, must be the perspective, the devotion the action, and the success the results, in perhaps many forms.

I knew that success needed a base, and I knew that the lack of a base was why I was having trouble here. But maybe it wasn't too late for me to still find my place, if only I could see more clearly. And there I began again. I kept setting up my conditions for what would let me settle into life; they were just an endless set of words to keep me content with discontent. I faded into the fog that came into my head each morning when I woke up, and I tried not to fight back against the heavy clouds too much. If I couldn't have my success, then why should I deny them theirs?

V.II

After They had the information They wanted, They had loosened up. They were too busy making plans of terror to think anymore on two abandoned prisoners, and Abigail and Grey found that they were not guarded so carefully as before. Just as quickly as this window of safety had appeared, he had helped her escape. She found that this had been his plan for a long time; he had simply needed to wait until the timing was right before acting. That was why he had not wanted to talk about escape before: he had known that the opportunity might come at some point, but only if they maintained secrecy about their plans. They could not act as if they had hope for breaking free, or perhaps their guard would never loosen up enough for them to leave. Grey had thought of all of this.

Once they had left behind the cells of darkness and foreboding sunrises, they had needed to move swiftly. Because going back to the city in the valley, or even near it, was no longer an option, he had shown her to the group of survivors in the wilderness. Grey had followed hidden paths and messages in the land that Abigail had not been able to see or decipher, bringing her finally to the camp. To feel welcome again, among these people, was like breathing in the sun. There was warmth all around, uniting everyone here in a sense of clarity; love grew tangibly among the members of this group, keeping them all safe. Even months later, Abigail kept close within her the memory of the day she had met them.

With the purveyors of darkness, with Them, the confines of space had been so cold, the air dead with dust. Lifeless in evil everything was, and good resolutions wavered and quaked. Yet as the pair spent the last day of their escape trip, life returned; the closeness of the land cleansed the dust from their eyes and brought resolution back into their limbs. As Abigail followed Grey silently through the rocks, the sun embraced them with arms of white heat. It didn't feel anymore as if she were making a desperate and dangerous escape: now her feet were moving in the rhythm of a dance, not a flight. The sun was her partner, so bold a presence that she could not ignore him, whether she chose to complain about the heat or to delight in it. Yet Abigail gladly accepted the brightness of the sun after the metal existence, so apart from everything natural, that she had survived during the past few weeks. Instead of scorching her limbs, the sun caught them up in his rays as he led her along; the light pounded into her skin, browning but not burning it. Abigail had never been one to burn in the sun; now as the warmth painted her skin darker, it also gave her strength for the long journey. She smiled up at the sky.

Only watching Grey bathed her smile once more in sorrow. His reaction seemed opposite to hers: while she thrived from freedom, he was haunted by what they had undergone. She was starting to let go of the terror now, but his face, unyielding in captivity, had broken the moment they had escaped. He had nothing left in this lonely state called freedom. Grey was a protector, which was what made him a good leader. Helping Abigail during their imprisonment had probably been a kind of relief to him, a way to save someone the way that he hadn't been able to save Alice. But now that he was entering the once safe and comforting expanse of his own lands, the lands not under Their possession, no doubt Alice was all in his mind once again. Alice should have been the one returning with him, and it was Alice he had not had the chance to save. Whether or not Abigail had also come, Alice should have been by his side. That was only right.

Abigail sighed. Grey looked back at her in concern, but she kept her face smooth, and he continued walking. The poor man, she thought. Even in his grief, he was so ready to move back into his role of helper if she needed him. It was his own sorrow he feared the most: he could comfort others, but not himself. Not right now. She wished she could share the sun with him; its golden light had already made her feel much better, though she didn't know how she could describe the effect out loud. Yet perhaps there was no need. Perhaps Grey did benefit from the sun's presence. Besides the joy, the clear light gave Abigail resolution, resolution to keep going even after everything had looked so bleak; the sun must also have given Grey the endurance needed for this task, for showing Abigail to her new home. Apart from his silence, he was still acting with strength, and that action was not negligible.

The only notice Grey had given Abigail was that they would arrive with the others on this day. He did not say at what time of day or where exactly they would find them, and perhaps he did not even know for certain. All that Abigail knew was that in the middle of the afternoon, they finished climbing across a series of hills and fell into a strange valley with dirt in shades of red and stark white. The vegetation was crustier here, with saguaros and green bushes filling in the land thickly. What with the cliffs and hills and mountains standing in all directions, the ground was still far from level, yet the little valley felt open. Openness would have been nice under any other circumstances, when space could be enjoyed without the constant need to hide away out of sight.

They found the survivors encamped by a tall promontory. It was an obelisk of raw earth and rock that grew from a sloping platform. More traditional cliffs stood behind it, offering the idea, at least, of protection within the small valley. If Abigail had not come here for a place of hiding, she would have found it intriguing, maybe beautiful. It was a quiet corner of adventures in white, red, brown, and green. But when she and Grey reached the camp, she cared very little about the traits of the valley anymore.

The beauty of the land fell into the background when she met the people who walked upon it and she cared only that she was among friends who automatically cared about her. They knew nothing about her and yet she could tell right away that they, like Grey, cared. As she walked among them, Abigail could also tell how pleased they were to find Grey again. He had always been one of the cause's most important figures, and he had been missing long enough to be considered lost. For them to discover that he had survived and had come back to them multiplied whatever hope they had saved. Such a miracle made Them appear to be a lesser threat and Grey to be a greater force of resistance.

The stragglers in the desert had a leader again, and they were glad. Not all of their plans had failed; not all of their number had been lost. The end to this chaos might, at last, finally be close. For one day, Abigail shared in their hope and saw no darkness.

V.III

I had Jesse and Sharon over Friday evening. At some point during the recent gap in my life, Jesse's newest book, which centered on Prescott's own Fort Whipple, had come out. This night was my way of finally congratulating him, belated though it was. Despite my good intentions, however, I felt more like it was an evening to lift up my spirits, not his. They were the ones asking me questions and trying to keep me entertained, though I was technically the hostess since this was my house. I didn't begrudge them the attempts, at least not at first: we had been through so much together that our friendship would not easily be abandoned.

Jesse and I had been friends since college, where we had both been history majors; he had been a couple of years ahead of me. I'd learned a lot from him, not just about study habits but also about his theory of study: he believed in focusing most on the places he lived in and around, hence the book about Fort Whipple. After college, we had stayed in touch over the years and the changing scenes: staying friends had always been important, first just to the two of us, and then to the four of us as couples. This transition had been fairly simple given that he had married Sharon not long before I married Nathan. We had often gone out for dinner together, or sometimes to a concert or for a hike. A few times, Sharon and I had gone shopping while Nathan and Jesse went golfing. I had laughed when Nathan beat Jesse by a fair number of points: my old college comrade didn't golf very often. Now, however, our even number of four was knocked down to three, one couple and one single instead of two pairs. The balance was gone, and I felt awkward, like maybe we didn't match anymore. Maybe, even if the friendship remained, everything we had once shared could no longer exist.

I looked over to my friends and considered them. Sharon wore a long, white cotton dress, nice yet casual; the bottom of the skirt had a green band with black embroidery that finished in thin ruffles, while more black edged the neckline. She finished with a pair of boots in black leather aged down to a rough texture. Boots were Sharon's signature piece; the only times I saw her without them were during her hiking escapades, which she planned quite frequently throughout the year. Jesse wore jeans in a dark wash that was almost brown and a green collared shirt. Probably Sharon had matched the color of the shirt to her dress; if I didn't love them, I would have envied the way they acted like a perfect, happy couple. Maybe I still did.

My own dress was plain black with a fifties style, A-line skirt. Indeed, like a good housewife out of the fifties era, I had made dinner for my friends tonight, even if I wasn't otherwise acting like much of a hostess. Salmon, golden potatoes, and cucumber salad with my usual iced tea were the evening's spread. I did often enjoy cooking, provided there was someone to cook for; food tasted better made at home and preparing it was a peaceful break from other tasks. Recently, though, I had grown a bit out of practice, hence the simplicity for today's menu. Sharon I allowed to bring the dessert, according to our usual tradition; she had baked a layered concoction of homemade brownie and pudding. We nearly finished it all just among the three of us.

After dinner, we moved into the living room and sat for some time, going over the details of our lives. It seemed a long time since we had sat together like this. Well, our group was together again, even if all of its members were not—and never would be anymore. And maybe it had been a long time: I didn't keep very good track of time anymore. Weekdays had significance in my life still because of work, but months did not. As the three of us talked, I imparted the latest news about the store. I told stories of some of the customers that had come through my doors; a few of them had asked silly questions and others had impressed me with their knowledge. I gave updates on notable pieces, telling whether certain items had sold yet or describing things that had just come in.

"Really, everything's been going just fine lately. There's so much going on what with the store and all that I hardly even have time to remember that anything is missing." That last part was true only in comparison to how I had felt before, when it was all so recent and crippling. But I was trying to mend the awkwardness I felt by telling these friends of mine that I didn't hurt anymore. I should've known that they didn't need me to lie, that lying would only make it all worse.

In reaction to what I had said, the structure in both their faces changed right before me. Eyes grew smaller, mouths became thinner, and lines began to appear on Jesse's forehead. I tried to impart my still limp and wavering optimism to them; I tried to make it seem stronger than it was. It didn't work. Instead of proving that I was fine, I ended up demonstrating the opposite: the words fell out of my mouth until I forgot what I was trying to say.

"This time of year is busy. You know how it is right now. The weather is nice, not as hot anymore but not cold yet, and Frontier Days is almost here, which always brings a lot of people. They're here more for the rodeo, but they come to the shop, too, when they're stopping by the Square. And I'm not just a cash register; I also have to chat with customers, give them directions—whatever they need. Today someone asked if there was a vegan café nearby, so I had to give her a couple of options, and yesterday everyone wanted to know if I sold umbrellas, which, of course, I do on rainy days. It all keeps me busy." Though everything I said was true, my tone grew exaggerated and they knew it. But I didn't want to admit, in front of them, that there was, after all, anything that filled my mind more these days than did the store. Frustrated that I was unsuccessful and tired with my efforts, I let my words turn. "Sorry there isn't anything more exciting going on that I can entertain you with."

Sharon, not wanting to make me feel bad, was quick to correct herself; I almost wished I hadn't turned on them. "It's not that, Julia. I know why you moved here and took over the store; I know what it all means to you, and I think I've always understood what's important to you and who you are. But do you?" She paused for half a beat. "What I mean is, don't ignore what you're going through because there's a reason you feel what you do and that's what you can't ignore. Don't forget what it makes you sad to remember. I know so much has happened that was never part of your plan, nothing you would have expected or ever wanted; it's hard, but you don't have to act as if it hasn't happened, especially with us."

"Well, I know that. But there's really nothing more for me to do. They're gone, and I'm stuck here. I'm the antique left behind, and if I choose to I can sit around trying to tell my story to anyone who will listen. But the thing is, not everybody who walks into an antique store wants to know all the stories. Sometimes people just want to create new stories with old things, and that's what I need to do. I can't try to tell the same story over and over again: it's over now and finished."

Sharon looked conflicted. She knew that I was, once again, telling the truth, but she also knew that I was still exaggerating. Whatever time had passed, however many months, and whatever I said I felt, I wasn't quite there yet emotionally; I couldn't set aside the story just yet. And whatever had physically ended would always remain in existence within my mind, even when I was ready to start a new beginning.

"Maybe," Jesse said, "you just need to take it slowly. Still go to work and everything, but come home and take time for yourself without feeling bondage, without trying to tell yourself that you need to be a certain way. Remember what you need to remember and feel what you need to feel: you have to let everything run its course. Admit that you miss them, and admit that your life will go on without them. Because, like you say, that story is over, and it will take you time to get used to the idea. After all, today is really only your first social get-together since. Right now is just the beginning." If he wasn't talking about the new beginning of resolution, then he meant the beginning of a new kind of difficulty, one different from the straight grief and crippling confusion I had already gone through, and that did not sound appealing.

I looked at the coffee table while I tried to think of a response. Even its dark, smooth wood now looked like it was choking, like my heart within me: the flat, rectangular top plunged downward into four spiraled legs, an elegant twist that I could only see as a pained contortion. The rocking chair where I sat was by the table's corner; the tufted leather sofa that Jesse and Sharon were sharing was parallel to the table and directly in front of the side window. It seemed a dangerous place to sit: maybe the outside air would suck them out at the bidding of the house, which wanted to keep me bound here to my loneliness. I almost wanted to let the house have its way so that I wouldn't have to play these games of healing anymore.

"Just be honest with us, Julia," I heard Jesse say.

"We can't offer you advice," Sharon said, "if you don't let us know what's really happening."

"Nothing's happening that I haven't already said, and I never asked for advice." Though I didn't want them to act as my counselors, I still instantly regretted the flakes of hot ashes that my words had thrown at them. "Look, I'm sorry. I guess I just know that it'll take a while, but that still doesn't help me in the meantime. I think it even makes it worse. I'll need your patience—again." Too many times.

"We'll be here, as many times as you need us," Jesse said. "Your friendship is still important, to both of us; that hasn't changed. And I want to thank you for having us over tonight. It may not have been easy, but it's good to get back into things. We'll make more plans again soon; we shouldn't forget each other."

"That's true." I lifted up my gaze. "Now who wants more tea?" I rose from my chair, uncertain if I was ending the conversation because I agreed with him or because I couldn't bear it any longer.

My head hurt. I had a near constant headache of blossoming closeness that pressed against every part of my mind. My head wanted to flee out of the pain and swirl away, even into nothingness. Yet I found no escape: there was nothing that I could do that would help. This was not the type of pain that I could soothe with medicine; it was more like the intangible ache that grew after working too hard for too long at math or some other mental exertion. But this was worse. This ache did not cease even if my mind rested; lack of rest was not the problem. Instead of ever ceasing, the headache maintained a constant biting feeling at the back of my head, all day and every day. With a tone dipped in fey humor, I called the gnashing teeth of pain a rat that made its life by sitting and chewing on the fibers of my head, snatching away my sanity.

This pain that I felt digging into me reminded me of heartbreak, or else the loss of a loved one. This pain was darkness, obscurity without clarity or comfort. A black forest, inescapable to travelers and going on without end, extended in my sight. The branches grew thorns right against my skin, ripping into my veins, and filled my footsteps with dead leaves and moss, never letting me see where I had stepped and stealing away any hope of removing myself from the tangles. When my feet tripped on the slippery leaves, dark mud covered my skin, sticking onto me and trying to glue me to the rotted ground. Not that it was much better when I could walk forward: I couldn't see where I was going and I couldn't trace my path. I feared I would never leave this place that hurt so much. No matter where I turned in the forest within my head, the pain sat like a covering of storminess all around me. Even if my mood was otherwise relatively content, which was sometimes the case, still the blackness pecked at me like unfinished business, demanding my attention and not letting me fall completely into peace.

I looked around, and I forgot to look ahead. I looked at me, and forgot that there was anything else. I looked at the forest in all its obscurity and I looked at my aching head. I absorbed it all and took it all into my veins, breathing the black blood into my lungs until I choked and coughed up more darkness. I couldn't think of anything besides the pain, and so that was all I let into my consciousness. Shadows were all that I could grow. On those occasional days of contentment, I lived only at the surface level and I did not gain anything or believe that any of the lightness could last. Those days might as well not have existed at all for all the good they did me: I began to realize that I didn't even try to fight for them to stay or to have meaning on my life.

Instead I sat, silently and unmoving, thinking that the rat in my head was only sleeping and would have to return eventually to feed on my mind and my blood. I accepted its future return readily because I couldn't imagine life without it, and in time I waited, each time that it slept, for it to come back. I was so smug as I waited for it that I was very nearly looking forward to the return, the return of pain though it was. Yet I bathed my pain and put it to bed, telling it to hush and sleep soundly until morning, when I would be there to greet it. I would wake it up again and sing it a song and carry it with me wherever I went, never letting it go. My beloved rat chewing away at the back of my head, why would ever I forsake you? What else is there besides pain to make me feel alive? I do so want to be alive, so I will be alive with you, if that is the only way that I can.

I hugged my headache so dear to me you'd think it was my way of healing my heartache, of embracing my pain until I could control it; you'd think control was my goal, though it was the furthest thing from my mind. You'd think that my skin and bones were made only of heartache, formed in perfect symmetry of darkness, and had always been so and would always be so. Yes, you would think so; everything made it seem so. I thought so. What other options were there?

VI.II

Even there, surrounded by friends and all their warmth, Abigail found herself just as haunted as Grey had been during their escape. The feeling of comfort she had found vanished too quickly. They both tried to go on as if nothing were amiss; after all, they had survived and safely gotten away. There was much to be glad about. But there were moments when the two of them were with the others and they caught each other's eyes within the group and knew that there was no more peace within them; the difference was too visible, too different from everyone else's expressions. They tried to shield the others from knowing the depth of their pain, but it was there all the same. It singled them out at one knowing glance. And it would always be there, even if they learned how to accept its existence.

That was what felt so strange to Abigail. She had always known that there was pain in the world, and she had felt some small measure of sorrow within her short life. But she had always viewed the world through light, and never had the darkness been so great as it was now. Still Abigail had hope and even joy what with the welcome from her new companions, but it was now joy comingled with desolation. She saw everything now, the light and the dark, and even when it was the light that was all around her, still she knew that the dark was there, also, hidden away somewhere in the world. And she could not escape it. And that haunted her, no matter how much she knew that the light would be the one to persist in the end. The end was not here yet, and Abigail wept for whatever time the darkness had left to rule upon the land. Knowing that the darkness had its reign and yet still living every day brightly, that was strange. It was just a touch away from being tragic.

Abigail wanted to remember what it was like before, when she had known light and dark only as abstract terms. Innocence, yes, that was what people called it; it was different from ignorance, which did not even know that light and dark existed. Although the people she was with now had probably had their own hardships and surely none of their eyes retained childhood innocence, still Abigail felt that the only one who could truly understand what she felt was Grey. No one else had been there with them through that time of captivity, so no one else understood what effect it had had on their minds. Whatever portion of horror the others had faced, it was not like the straightforward reality that Abigail had seen. She had seen the lid of evil lift and expose human hearts jumping willingly into muddy water and suffocating themselves, abandoning all roots of life. Her hope, which had been forced to persist through this experience, was grown different and more painful than theirs. Her hope knew the depth of sorrow and was now glimpsing the depth of joy. She didn't know how much further that depth went or what formed its boundaries. She only knew that it took more strength to carry this ever-widening perspective.

So every day Abigail walked with heavy hope and haunting memories. Never did the weight of pain leave her. It was there when Abigail, curled up on the ground beneath a blanket, could not sleep at night and stayed awake staring up at the dusty stars. It was there when, after the waking hours of the day were spent once more, she watched the orange sun fade into the land's flesh at sunset. Like a ball of neon blood, it spurted out across the clouds into a veil of darkened light. Blood, she learned, was the precursor to the night of shadows. By blood, the sunlight left to give the dark its domain. But it was also by blood that the weary were given rest. Night was a gift, the time given for the world to escape for a moment from sorrow and exertion, yet Abigail could share in that rest only if she could wipe the blood off of her eyesight. She could not sleep with the veil of red in her eyes that threatened to burn into her soul.

During the daylight hours, Abigail brought her arm to her forehead to wipe away the sweat formed by the sun. She wished, as she felt the moisture sliding away from her skin, that the sight of blood was as easy to lift away. The sweat was easier to live with because it was only a physical hindrance. The pain of blood, however, constantly soaked her visage, and she could not wipe it away. It became her blood and also Grey's blood and the blood of every person who had been captured and had cried out for mercy. Blood had poured over them all in darkness, until their own blood came out and brought the light to cover the dark. But by then everything was red, and Abigail was in shock and could distinguish nothing anymore. She did not know what she saw in these veins built by sorrow; it was a terrifying mass of brightness where one piece bled into another and a single tremble reverberated all the way across to the opposite side.

She walked across the earth and found the blood everywhere, even in peaceful places. It was there in the deep red dirt that she had nearly admired as beautiful, in the sharp lines of the mountains that she had once found protecting, in the needles of the plants that helped them live, and in the whites of her own eyes that blinked only in pain. Everyone said that her eyes were just colored in red because she was scared, sad, and tired; they would turn clear once more. Abigail knew better. While it was true that she was tired, the clear whiteness could never return. Because Abigail had felt the essence of sorrow, fear, and exhaustion, right down to the very center of darkness, the red blood had stained the whiteness of her eyes in permanency. If ever the red cleared, still the eyes would never be the same. And neither would be Abigail the guardian of these eyes.

Desolation entraps the weary, this she had seen, and from whence, Abigail wondered, do they make their way back into the light? If the blood or horror could never fade, what then would enable her to live with the persisting redness?

VI.III

Even though I was learning to soldier on when I was around people, it was turning frustrating to be alone. Frustrating wasn't even quite the word I wanted; what I felt was the battle between what I ought to do and what I could do. When I was alone, the gap between these two sides grew greater before my eyes. I could see an image of myself accepting my new life and becoming a flowery person who volunteered for the town and always helped out friends and never felt lonely or regretful. But the real image was still too broken and confused to reach out to that reality or bring it into even partial reality. I hated to be still, and I hated to be in a single space, and yet that was all there was for me every morning and every evening. My head pounded beneath the captivity.

I was so aware of the boundaries that made up my house, my dream house though it was. Every wall I could feel, and every window seemed too small, every door too shut. I had etched my heart into this home when I moved in, remembering every curve and loving every corner, and now when I tried to distance myself from the building, it was too late. I found that my bones were already soldered onto the wooden frame and its fate would be my fate: if it ached in emptiness, then so would I. Rising from my bed in the morning, moving from the library to the kitchen, or walking in the front door, I felt my body creak with each step over the squeaky hardwood floor with an uncanny harmony. And I didn't know what to do.

I could hardly step outside: other than work, I had nowhere to go. At least, there was nowhere that I could stay very long and nowhere that I wanted to be. I spent my social time at the shop, and I was enjoying it again, but that was enough for now. Anything more I could not bear: casual conversations could still hurt for no real reason and crowds made me feel alone. I didn't want to try any harder than I needed to, and Jesse had advised me to come home and take time for myself, anyway. That was what I was doing. But it didn't seem to be helping. I would go insane shut up inside here, and that couldn't be the effect he'd wanted. Locked within the walls of my beloved house, I would explode, my mind filling up every vein of my body with a solid substance until my skin burst from my bones and my thoughts took up their place in the exposed air.

But if I, too, became part of the air, where then would be what was left of my family? Completely gone we would all be, first one, then two, and then the last one. Bound once by blood, we would be bound by ephemeral air and my bodiless mind, which had not waited for its natural separation from the world, would be lost, unable to find them. I didn't want an eternal separation for us. So here I stayed, alone, knowing here I would probably stay for years and more years before my time came to leave. It could be a very long wait before I saw them again, a long time to spend without them.

What I did want for my family in this world, however, was gone away, so perhaps nothing mattered anymore. Nathan and I had planned to live in this house until we were too old and tired to climb the stairs. Charlotte I had hoped would inherit the home, or perhaps by then she would have children of her own and one of them might want to keep it, if she had already made a home elsewhere. But I was all this house had left now, and I had no family to leave it to. There were very few relatives, only distant ones I stayed in sparse touch with. They had their own lives apart from mine. After me, this house would be empty, left for some stranger to come in and take over. And not only would Charlotte not inherit the home but she would also would never even grow up; I had lost both her and Nathan, as I had lost Andrew years before, and that was too much. The loss of Andrew, who had never lived in this house, had been part of the reason why I had moved to Prescott to build a new life where sorrow was more distant. If I acted now as I had done before when faced with loss, I would run away once more, start over once again. It had helped last time. Prescott had been good for my family for several years, until one irresponsible driver had ruined it all.

I was tempted, because of how painful this house had become to be in by myself, to run from my loss one more time.

But that couldn't be the right path. I didn't want to run anymore: running was in itself tiring, even if it could somehow obliterate all grief. And though I was just coming into my fifties, it seemed too late to start my life over entirely. Maybe I hesitated because, unlike before, I didn't have Nathan with me this time. This time, if I ran, I would be starting over by myself. There would be no one to share the struggle with, no one to lean on, and no single strong thread back to the life I had fled. Or maybe the reason I hesitated was because I was established here. I already had a house, a job, friends, everything I needed right here— except for what I wanted, of course. That was my family.

I tried to make the house my own, since it was no longer theirs. It was time to admit at least that much. Maybe if the house, to which I was so bound, moved on, then I would be able to, as well.

On the hooks in the entranceway where their jackets had hung, I placed a couple of my hats. I put some of my favorite books on the side table where Nathan had kept his current reading material. I took away their toothbrushes, lotions, and combs from the bathroom, filling in the empty space with handmade soaps and other trinkets. On a daily basis, I used to keep only three placemats on the table because there were only three of us and it seemed unnecessary to set out any more. Now I kept a placemat for every chair. I could no longer have three because there were no longer three people living here, and just one for me seemed too somber, so a complete set it would be. That made visual sense.

All of these things were all of the easy things.

Harder to deal with than things were time and space. Nothing was the same anymore, and perhaps I felt so alone because every decision was now all my own, unhindered by other opinions and other needs. How I missed the hindrances. I felt confused, not having to wake up early enough for breakfast before driving Charlotte to school. My car was bored driving straight to work without the detour, short though it had been. My body became lonely when it knew there was no reason to rush home at the end of the day because there was no one there waiting for me. The house felt boxy with only me, occupying only one room at a time; all the empty rooms stared at me, wondering why they were alone, so much space built for people but without any people to enjoy it.

I listened and heard only myself. I looked and no one was there. I waited and no one came.

There were no music lessons to take her to on Thursdays, no friends' houses to pick her up from. There were no family nights watching TV together on Sundays, having dinner on the sofa while trying not to spill anything. There were no more dinners out, just the two of us, on the occasional Friday. There was nothing for me to do anymore, and everything that I did do seemed to take less time. Dinner and dishes and cleanup for one person and still there were hours left before bed. I read and I redecorated and I paced, and still I found myself in this locked tower of a beautiful house. I missed my old house, which was the same house, just my house when I had felt happy sitting in it. The difference was tangible.

This house was not the same anymore, not really. This house echoed in hollowness. There was no music coming out of Charlotte's room, no sound of sports channels coming from the TV Nathan was watching, and no one to call out to when it was time to eat or to leave somewhere. Footsteps drifted only from my shoes and there was no rustling from a distant corner because I was the only one here to make any sounds. Only the walls watched me and listened to me, and my words died as soon as they touched the flat wood. The wood could not answer me, and its silence tormented me. It was silence where once there was much life. Everything had changed now.

My house of dreams caved in around me.

VII.I

I felt as if I were struggling against my entire body, even the intangible mind. I was neither sore nor stiff, yet there was heaviness in my shoulders, arms, and legs; it made me feel so tired. That made it difficult to want to do anything that I did not need to do, and so I did very little, probably neglecting many possibilities. Home and work, with my idle walks, and that was all; I went nowhere else and I did nothing else. Yet my body felt like it belonged to a very busy and athletic person: I was always tired and thirsty. Though I kept drinking water, I never felt that I was hydrated enough. My mouth could think of nothing but water but the water did not satisfy. The liquid slipped down my throat again and again without seeming to make any difference: I remained dry and the sides of my mouth continued to beg for more. Maybe I could have simply been sick, except for the fact that my mind was a part of this battle. That meant that it was something more, something that caught up both sides in one struggle to bring me down.

My mind, captured inside my head, swung back and forth, whirling in both emotion and thought. Moving round and round above my shoulders, my head felt magnetized to the floor, as if it would sink down from one angle or another and hit itself and close my eyes in a faint. In reality, gravity kept my head steady and straight, but I wondered if maybe it would be easier to just give in to the mad magnet's pull. I was so tired. My mind felt too fragile to go on without a seven days' sleep, and I imagined that it would eventually claim that sleep for its own, no matter what I did to try and stop it. At some point, I would slip and make a mistake. And so to everything that I did, just the simplest of tasks, I had to give double or triple focus, trying to compensate for my confused and heavy mind. If I did not, the magnetic pull would take over and I would reel downwards in mind and body, falling paralyzed to the world.

And I had no desire for that. I did not hate the world or my life; I wasn't living in so much bleakness as that, otherwise I wouldn't have cared whether or not I was achieving anything here. In fact, a part of me, if only a small part, felt rather well. I could still see positivity. This world had potential, even for such as me, and there were things here that even I appreciated. Certainly I didn't feel like fainting away from everything that I knew and everything that I lived within; it would be harder to once again face something new than to stay here with what was relatively familiar. I was beginning, though terribly slowly, to accept this place as my home, and no one willingly leaves home behind without reason. It was simply the matter of knowing how to fit myself to this territory that kept me down. I wanted to do well, but every time that I pictured doing well, it was not really me that I saw; it was another person, one that I didn't know how to become.

Was it my spirit, then, that had good intentions, while the chemical side went about wallowing in its convulsions of weakness? That might explain much. If I could just end this thirsty heaviness in my body, then could I take control? Could I blame it all on my body's weakness? That was a tempting conclusion. But even if the blame passed away from me, that did not help much: I would still have the same problem, just with a different reason. All that would help would be for this weakness to be an illness rather than a choice: then all I would have to do would be to wait it out, to amble through the piles of days without doing anything differently. The thought of waiting for change without working toward it was appealing; probably most of my days that was exactly the course I took. Except, of course, for when my head wavered so heavily and my limbs were so tired that I didn't even want to get up from my desk at lunchtime. Then I wanted a way out.

VII.II

Abigail sat on the ground with her knees up by her chest; she gazed upward toward the sun, leaning her head back and half closing her eyes. She let the golden light fade through her eyelids and absorb all the way into her head, her heart, and her soul. Trying to forget for a moment that she was flesh and blood, she wished for the simplicity of the natural world around her. Abigail's wish became words that she barely knew she was speaking, so absorbed was she in her dream. Though she made barely a sound, the words fell into the clay of the land and their tremor drifted toward the sky.

"Take me. Let me be free; why am I held down like this? Why don't you make me to sway in the breeze as the plants do? Why am I not made to survive so straightforward as the saguaro do, year after year? I want to be the wind, who can float above the earth and spread only life, not pain, as it flies across endless expanses, always finding a new view of beauty. Why must I instead be in this weak body that, even when I tell it to embrace its place, still pants at the heat, grows dizzy, and sweats for mercy? I was fine, truly I was, but it was the body that failed me. Its blood and tears won't let me go on; they are all I can see and they have chased away my lightness of spirit. Why couldn't I have a more reliable frame?"

"Abigail." The obtrusive voice spoke quietly.

"What." She didn't want to bother giving the word the enunciation of a question: she was annoyed that someone had been a part of her confession.

"Tired though your body may be, we must move on. They're waiting." Ah, it was Grey, then, who spoke; she recognized his voice now, beckoning her back to the crowd so that they could continue their journey. Abigail could hardly begrudge Grey knowing her thoughts; secrets between them no longer made sense after what they had been through together. But maybe he had not heard everything: it was not simply that Abigail was tired from walking and living constantly under the desert sun. She was also weary from the pictures of pain her eyes kept feeding her, the memory of trauma that had settled into her brain. And the worry that it was not yet over.

"Come." He held out his hand to help her up. So she had to let the moment fade and follow him away, letting go of her longing and her mind's plea. She had not, in any case, succeeded in escaping from where she was, so it was just as well to leave be the dream. But Grey's hand was comforting; standing up again, next to him, no longer seemed as impossible a thing to ask. Grey's spirit was trapped in a body just like hers, and yet this appeared to pose no problem to him. He struggled, but he always looked in control of his struggle. Abigail realized that he might be able to pass the root of his strength on to her.

"Grey," she asked as they began moving, "do you ever . . ." She sighed. "Get frustrated by the way we have to live? I mean, in human bodies and all their weakness. Sometimes it seems like we have control over so little." Maybe she had been wrong to ask this, especially now. She still barely knew Grey, and this was a personal question, in more ways than one. Grey was always so comfortable in himself, but there would be more than only himself in his thoughts right now. The body of Alice, his other half, had just been destroyed on this earth; he would still be grieving for her. Maybe now was not the time to remind him of the impermanency of dust.

"Yes." Clear and adamant he spoke, yet the single word was followed by a pause of some steps. These steps, which they took to move from one place to another, were yet another disadvantage to which physical reality held them. Their need or desire to move always had to wait on time and effort. The time that it took to walk the length of a path raced against the energy left in weakened bodies. So not every person made it to the next destination, and some gave up as soon as they had begun. The expending of energy, that was life. And the loss of energy, that was death.

Grey lifted his head toward the sky, as if he were checking the sun's position. Or maybe he just needed time to choose his words and compose his face. He closed his eyes for a moment before turning to look at Abigail. Though his gaze appeared resigned, the components of Grey's face fell wearily. Abigail wasn't used to seeing him this way.

"I think to myself that if only Alice had been in a less destructible shell, she would still be here with me. If we had been formed of eternity from the start, there would be no separation. But that isn't the point of anything. Right now, she's more alive than ever she was when I knew her. Mourning losing her is enough; I can't also mourn that it was possible for death to rip her away from me. I wouldn't gain anything from that, nor would anyone. We just have to accept what the world around us is and do our best the way we are, with what we are given." He looked down toward the ground.

"I'm sorry." Seeing his questioning gaze, Abigail added, "To bring up Alice, that is. I didn't mean to hurt you." She had only been thinking of herself, expecting him to be stronger than her just because she hadn't seen the pain hidden away. Now she hated to think that she had stirred that pain.

Grey smiled and closed his eyes again.

"Abigail, there is nothing you or anyone else can do to hurt me now. Since my heart has survived this much, I think it must be impermeable stone. You come to me for advice, but it seems I have none left to give. I'm only half myself anymore, and I don't think this world will give me time enough to recover. I'm floating down a stream toward rolling rapids—and beyond, roaring falls that even a stone can't survive."

Abigail's gaze fell. She had gained neither hope nor comfort from the conversation, not because Grey had offered her none, as he had said, but because she had seen that he suffered even worse than she did in this life. She could not focus on his words of comfort because of his confession of fear. If he, who was always so strong, felt pain and sorrow, then from these none could escape. And where did that leave the world?

No one was safe from sorrow; only the recovery of hope would save them. Abigail walked on quietly.

VII.III

It was ten o'clock; I had told them ten o'clock. They would be here. They had no reason not to come. I was prepared. They would be prepared. I set my foot on the sidewalk bordering the Courthouse Square and started walking. They may have been having trouble finding a close parking space; it was ten o'clock on a Saturday, after all. A little early still, perhaps, but not so early that no one was out yet: this area was popular both for shoppers and people simply wanting to walk about and enjoy the day. Many brought their dogs with them; there were usually several four-legged creatures out at a time. I checked the time on my phone. 10:01. So I was the late one. Maybe they were already here waiting for me, worried that I had changed my mind.

I turned the corner onto the west side of the Square. About half a dozen cars away, parked in one of the spaces along the curb, was their SUV; standing in front were Jesse and Sharon, looking as if they had just stepped out. We must have both arrived at about the same time. I didn't know why I had worried so much about timing, anyway. It wasn't as if it would have made a difference if one of us had needed to wait a few minutes for the other.

"Julia! Glad you could make it," said Jesse. Of course I could make it: as I had assured him when he'd invited me, I had nothing else to do and needed only fight with my reluctance to begin behaving like a regular person again. I was certain I had forgotten how to do everything except clean the house and run the store. Jesse knew I was having trouble; that was why he acted so excited to see me, as if his upbeat mood would raise my own. If only it worked that way. Instead I think he just made me feel more aware of my somber attitude—and therefore feel more awkward.

I was not sure what to think even now, as we all got into the car to drive to the trailhead. We had driven out for hikes dozens of times before, but this was the first time it would be just the three of us; I was still adjusting to the odd number. I tried not to look at the vacant seat next to me, thinking instead of the route the car was taking. Today's trail was fairly long, so we were planning to only go up to the summit and come back down. Probably if it were just the two of them, they would have started earlier and gone through the whole trail. But they were trying to make my first outing easy. After all, emotional well being aside, even the physical aspect might have some challenge to it: I couldn't remember the last time I had gone on a hike. I climbed all the stairs in my house multiple times a day, but that was about all the exercise I'd had in months.

As we drove, we passed through Mt. Vernon Avenue: it was not exactly for ease that I had asked them to meet me at the Square instead of picking me up at home. I had given the excuse that I wanted to check in with my assistant, Carol, at the store before taking the weekend off; I had visited her and gone over a few things, but I hadn't really needed to. What I had wanted was to walk the short distance from my house to meet them so that I could separate myself from this my world of dreams before beginning the new day. Mt. Vernon was a dream now, a dream I'd thought I had fulfilled years ago. But what did people do when solid dreams crumbled? Dreams I had always thought we needed; I had believed in their power and I had made them transition into reality. But what did all my dreams mean now, now that death had killed these my dreams?

When our car pulled into an empty parking space at the trailhead, I glanced at myself in the side mirror, more to take up a moment of time than to check my appearance. Yet once I had observed the reflection of my face, I had to pause to look harder: there was something there that I had not expected. There were my green eyes, my slightly tanned skin, and the light brown hair growing on the edges; there, too, was a fairy spark. It might have simply been the reflection of the light in my eyes, reminding me of sparkling pixie dust, yet I had thought I was already dead along with my dreams and long past any glittering reflections. From where came this spark of life if not from me? Everything about my face looked healthy, so unlike the pallor of grief I'd been expecting. The glow of color around my cheekbones seemed to match my eyes more prominently than ever. My hair did not look colorless or unkempt; it looked like a living part of me, a brush of softness like a smile beneath a straight face. Though I had applied no makeup to my lips, they were bright. It couldn't be with happiness—so what was it, then? Something was keeping me alive even in my grief.

I made my observations quickly, growing embarrassed as I remembered that I was not alone and that I had just professed to these two friends that I was the same as I had always been. Acting surprised at my own face would not help my claims. But maybe I had been exaggerating less than I'd thought when I'd said I was okay. Maybe I was, after all, more unchanged than I imagined. Maybe grief wasn't a new phase of my existence; maybe it was just another emotion through which I would have to make passage. So long as both my friends and I knew of this passage through darkness, perhaps it was fine if I acted a bit off, staring at my face in the mirror or not making much conversation. At least they knew why I was acting different from my usual self, and at least they were here with me as I made my way through this.

I got out of the car, smoothing out my shirt as I did. The thick cotton material was green; my pants, an old pair of jeans I'd kept on as outdoor clothes, were a worn blue. My shoes looked like brown Mary Janes from the top, though the thick black soles gave away the fact that they were designed for hiking. I wore my hair in a ponytail, as I usually did for hikes, and the style felt uncomfortable because it had been so long since I'd worn it. Though my hair was not long enough that it fell past my shoulders when it was loose, still my head felt exposed without my hair waving about my face and neck. I felt like, along with my every expression, my every thought would be on display this way. There would be no more secrecy left.

We made our way up to the trailhead, talking very little for a time. Jesse and Sharon were giving me space and I was taking it. It was easier to say nothing than to say things I didn't mean. And it was difficult right now to even know what to say, especially out here in the open with no walls to muffle my complaints. I worried I would disturb the forest with my inner tumult. There was such silence here; the difference between this silence and the silence of my house was absolute.

"Look at that." Sharon said when we were nearly at the top. She pointed to a bare patch in the trees, where a young tree was beginning to grow. "For as long as I've been coming up here, nothing has grown there."

"It's a tree growing, Sharon. It happens." She seemed too excited for one tree; I could tell she was about to make a metaphor and I really didn't want to hear it. I hadn't come out here just for all the focus to be about how I needed time in order for my life to begin again.

"Life can always start anew," she said. "Nothing's so solid that we can't change it for the better."

Despite my reluctance to listen to metaphors, she had left me unable to answer. There was something about how she had worded her sentence that made me pause. Solidity. Change. Ability. Strength. The words floated loose in my head. And since I was so unsure of what I was thinking that I didn't know what to say, I gave especial concern to my footfalls instead. In fact, now was the time to take extra care where I stepped: we were approaching the lookout spot on the summit where the path was steep and ended in a vertical fall downwards. If I was not careful, my present confused and distracted state of mind, without thinking, might tumble my body over the edge.

I looked up and out and saw colors of green and blue. Layers of pine trees folded themselves outward from where we stood, giving way to ripples of hills; mountains outlined the background. Builders had positioned neutral-colored houses in some of the hills; these houses, designed simply as dwellings, now became part of the landscape. For being regular houses, they fit in remarkably well. Open space on the surfaces of the hills reflected against soft texture and everywhere the colors came together in one smooth wave. There was something in that view. In my bones I felt it. A new echo of familiarity ran through my veins, and I listened to the silence of the hills now almost with joy.

After staying a moment, we turned to go back down the path. Jesse gave me his hand to help me over a boulder; I stepped carefully down from the rock's bulk, which had not felt as steep on the way up. The feel of the ground, always waiting there beneath my feet, was a comfort during these rocky sections. I felt like the earth was accepting me and bidding me a good journey across its landscape. Looking about at the pine trees, I pictured their personalities and watched their stories unfold while I walked by. Trunks lifted out of the dry ground and stood up in guardianship of their world. Their branches reached out toward one another, and though most of them did not physically touch, their graceful gestures were their inner conversations. Young trees were there and old trees were there. Green needles clothed their bodies, while birds were the eyes in their branches. With the trees we walked, growing ever closer to the foot of the hill; my body felt healing and wondered when my mind would come to

join it.

VIII.I

I woke up one morning in blank shock. My dreams. What were they? How had they turned on me so suddenly? Sleep was supposed to bring rest and refreshment, not this. The first part of the night had been comfortable enough; I had no awareness of anything in it that had not been smooth and silent. I had woken up early in the morning and let myself fall asleep again briefly until it was a more reasonable hour. There was nothing unusual about that. But when I woke for the second time, my internal world was changed, shredded by my dreams into a box of fright with windows of darkness and a door I didn't want to touch.

I had to hold my body still and dared not move, not my arms or legs or even my eyes; if I moved, the fright of the dreams might move from the past back into the present. I might stir something that I never wanted to see again. I stayed this way, completely still, for a few moments just to try and keep my sanity, to try and tell myself that dreams had no bearing on reality. Dreams never made me scream and I did not scream now, but these dreams, they had done something to me. If the thought of screaming, so different from what I usually did and from the utter stillness I woke up to, had even occurred to me, this time I would have screamed. If ever a dream were to wake with a scream, this would have been it.

I had never been truly traumatized. So I didn't have that kind of an experience to remember and use for comparison. But that's what it felt like, this waking. They were not typical nightmares I had had; instead, they were painful thoughts born out of the guise of dreams. They tore into all my notions of safety, comfort, peace, and everything else that protected the mind from shock and insanity, from trauma. Perhaps they were based on real worries that I had, and that was what made them so frightening? Or had something evil touched my dreams? I didn't know and I couldn't guess: I remembered only the shadow of a fragment of what I had dreamt. It was horror; I could recognize that much, even if I could not identify what exactly had caused it or why.

Whatever the case, adjusting to this fright in my mind took time. Even once I was able to sit up in bed, I had to wait a bit longer before I could move more; my limbs were still in shock. Then, in a sudden burst of terror, I pulled back the blankets and fled. I had to leave this room entirely. It felt uncomfortable, touched by whatever had been in those dreams, and I couldn't quit the space quickly enough. It was my only chance of separating myself from that feeling. As I sat in the kitchen, however, I thought warily of the bedroom where my dreams had visited me, still there just beyond the wall even though I was no longer in it.

And I couldn't bear it.

I started crying. I thought of my dreams that I could barely even remember, I thought of the house that I was having trouble being in, I thought of the people I knew who had been in my dreams, and I wept. And I sobbed. I touched the tears with my fingers, wondering what was this strange heartbreak that had come on me from nowhere. These tears felt more like blood than any others, more like they'd been ripped out of my arteries by some unnatural means. Then my face was entirely in my hands, the air choking in and out of my throat. I was being strangled by this horror without even knowing what it was. I was glad at least that I was the only one there and that no one could see me right now in such breathless fear. This moment felt so apart from everything tangible that I wanted no tangible witnesses to its existence.

Though I soon had to get myself ready and begin going about my day, it was a couple of hours before I was able to feel somewhat normal again. Even then, I could not entirely be rid of the dark feeling. It was a bleak pain trying to grip my head and arms, to carry me away by my shoulders. I tried to continue on, anyway, though I wondered if I had overlooked something or failed to receive important news. I worried that someone or something, my acquaintances or even the world, had suffered. Maybe, I worried, there was something wrong that I was feeling before the actual news of it came. Then I worried about going back to sleep that night.

First I had feared the world around me and then I feared the world in dreams. None of this was helping, and with each new fear, I could only imagine a thousand more coming my way. Every new world of fearful realities pushed me further away and deeper into my own isolated bed of worry.

VIII.II

Illuminant light. Life is light. The words drifted through Abigail's mind as she slept. She was stretching out her arms straight in front of her while she sat on the edge of a rocky cliff; the land dug deep down beneath the cliff before rising again into a line of mountains. Between the ending and the beginning, the fall and the rising, that was where she sat. She bent forward her body in an appeal to the land, letting its sense of being take over her limbs and forgetting all her past in favor of this one moment. She was edging further out into the open; her limbs felt heavy yet she did not feel as if she were bearing all of their weight. Her legs hung out over the cliff, one bare foot falling straight down to caress the stone and also to hold her balance; the other leg she held horizontal, its foot reaching out to meet with her hands far away from the edge. Abigail folded her body outward, arms against leg, foot and hands together, reaching to the horizon.

The sun was brilliant. Abigail felt it absorbing into her skin. All the while she sat under its gaze, it warmed and tightened her skin, the living leather that covered all of her limbs. As soon as sweat formed from all of the heat, it evaporated back into the air, yet still the moisture kept her skin from drying out or turning to flame. So it was that the sun burned her while also imbuing her with the power to be burnt without burning. The glare was all white and never charred like ashes. So great were the sun's white illuminations that it soon became too hot and bright to see by. Everything in Abigail's view was soon glowing and indistinguishable and it hurt her eyes to look about. Finally the glare made her shut her eyes, and a new image grew on the closed eyelids, as though she had fallen into another layer of sleep.

She had a dream. She saw Alice and Grey walking together beneath willow branches. All was green, and the very ground beneath them was lush; the foliage gave under their footsteps as softly as layers of sea foam. At intervals, the pair would turn to each other and smile as they walked in a steady and rhythmic pace. But before them was a land of red. Volcanoes, miniature in size as trees, burst from the ground and gave forth vaporous, burning blood. The lava came soon to flow across all the land, but into its midst Alice and Grey continued to walk. The redness touched their feet. But it didn't swallow them. It rushed about like gore, but they floated upright in it, maintaining the constancy of their walk. Their ankles disappeared after their feet, then their knees, and so on until nothing but their smiling faces were left on this earth.

Then this, too, vanished. Abigail's eyes turned white and the land of red fell out of focus and she saw Alice, with Grey, standing somewhere within her new vision's grasp.

She had a dream that the earth exploded and that life did not end. She had a dream of what persisted past the end of all things.

Abigail awoke abruptly. The layers of dreams were all gone, and she knew she was back to the waking world, where dawn was ready to rise. The land was very nearly cold against her skin after all of the lights of red and white that she had dreamed. Though such strange dreams of light and shadow worried her, Abigail saved the dreams for pondering. For now she needed to rise and investigate the stirring that she felt in the camp: footsteps were pressing into the ground around her, yet it was too early for the usual start to the day. There was hardly any light out; the small shreds of it stretched like shadows on the land. The sky was gray. Usually everyone waited to rise until the sun itself reached the horizon. The early movement must have meant that Grey and the others were returning from their foray away from the main group; they had left to find supplies and scout the surrounding area.

Eager to see Grey again, Abigail went out with the rest of the group, hurrying in the direction they all faced. She found herself standing on an outcropping of rock, looking down. There was a silent questioning in the air around her, something confused instead of excited in the conversation. Abigail, suddenly afraid to ask anyone what was happening, edged towards the front of the group.

She set her eyes toward the horizon. There, walking steadily towards her, were the five figures. Five was exactly the number she had expected to see: it was five men who had set out a few days ago. But where was the shorter figure? Abigail knew that the other men who had gone were taller than Grey, but none of the approaching figures stood out as shorter than the others. She wondered if they were standing on uneven ground that made their heights appear the same; after all, this land was full of hills and rocks with very little flatness. Surely Grey was among them and she just couldn't distinguish him from here. Her perspective was just distorted. Surely. Abigail could accept nothing else.

They could not have lost one of their leaders in so routine a trip; they never lost anyone this way, and out of everyone he could not be the first. Lost in the desert, forgotten as outcasts, they could not also lose him. They needed him. He could not be gone. He was their leader; he gave them hope and guidance, united them and helped them plan. What could they achieve without him? What could Abigail do without him? She needed someone who could understand her; she needed the person who had helped her live. And if he was gone, then who could be the fifth person? There was no one missing from the group here, and what were the chances that they had found another survivor in the forgotten places of the desert? Were there even any others left? Surely, somehow, it had to be Grey after all.

VIII.III

"The last rose."

The day being pleasant and mild, I had taken myself out to tend to the roses. Roses always seemed like classic flowers:

they were as suitable today as they had been to the Victorians and were therefore a perfect complement to my house's front yard. A Victorian rose garden did make the most sense for a Victorian house, even if there were so many other flowers in the world to choose from. Although hearty as flowers went, especially considering how long these had been growing here, the roses were not immune to ill. That was the reason for my sorrowful proclamation: one of the plants wasn't doing well. Maybe it was just falling into winter hibernation early, but I hated to see the color leave. Winter made healthy plants look dead and, for those without fall colors, took away all their flowers. From this bush bloomed a single rose, sprouting from a spiny branch. The thorns, dark brown, pricked out from the branches and threatened the one rose lest it linger too long after all the others were gone. Its remaining time was scarce.

As I spoke out, I pressed my fingers toward the petals, unsure whether to pick the flower or to leave it be. It would not last long either way, whether it withered on the branch or off; I didn't know which would be better, so I stood staring at the pale rose and wondering what to do or why it even mattered. I never had trouble cutting flowers when there were many on each bush, but everything seemed different with only one left. It looked so soft there, and I knew that it would soon die, anyway, if I did not cut it off. But should I let it await its natural death rather than take it away now?

A child, in a harsh world of thorns—was it better off nesting in its parents' arms or leaving the shadowlands for the light?

"Was my child better off leaving me, first one and then the other? Was Nathan also?" I was acting like Sharon with her nature metaphors.

Instead of staying focused on the symbolism of death, I wondered whether it was sadder that Nathan had lived half a life in happiness with me, or that Andrew and Charlotte had never had the opportunity to begin their adult lives. Maybe it was worse to abruptly leave a full life, to see what that tasted like and to leave it unfinished. But it always seemed so tragic for life to end almost as quickly as it had begun. That's what everyone told me, that it was so sad that they had missed out on so many experiences, that they had never even reached adulthood. Both of them. People always seemed more struck by the death of children.

But Nathan had reached adulthood. He had grown up and fallen in love and made a career and started a family and built up a whole life only to leave me with aching grief and an empty house with no husband and no children—and that was sad. The more we had together, the more we had to lose when the time came. Sometimes I almost wished that I had never known any of them, these three most important people in my life, so that I would have lost none of them. It was the loss of two generations, the father and the children, with only me left as a disjointed ghost to act as caretaker to the abandoned shell of a home that death had left behind as a forgotten remnant of life. I felt like my very being meant nothing anymore without them, as if they were all that defined me.

The roses grew their thorns to keep me locked up in hopelessness and the absence of all hints of warm color, and unlike the plants I was granted no gift of sleep to await the beginning of a new season. This year winter would not be kind to me as it had once been: winter would only mean consciously staring at the thorns around me every day and waiting until they blossomed anew. I would wait this year so longingly for spring to cover up all shades of winter. The weather, though, was barely beginning its transition into fall; still there was a long winter of many dormant days ahead of me, days that I would probably not be able to count or track in any way.

I closed my eyes to picture the four of us together again, together in a way that had never been and never would be. Nathan and I had paler and thinner hair and more wrinkles on our faces. Andrew was tall; his smile was just as I remembered, except that it came from a man instead of a small child. Charlotte stood next to him, smiling with him the way they used to as children, the way she had never been able to smile again after she lost him. If I imagined a few more years passing, they would each be married and four people would turn to six; the number might increase still more with grandchildren coming into the image.

Family would no longer be narrow and cold; it would be wide and warm, too ever present to fade away. I smiled at the scene, delighting in the idea; I would not have been able to do this a few months ago.

But now I was learning the difference between regretting and imagining. I could not regret the lives cut short. But I could imagine, just for the pleasure of it, what it would have been like for things to happen differently. I wasn't trying to flee from reality, but picturing that imaginary future did help to lessen the pain of real memories. It helped me to realize that, however life ended, I did not regret its duration. If they had all lived on for many more years, they would have also experienced more pain and sorrow; every life, no matter what length, contains both. And the joyful moments out of the past are so much more savory to remember than the dark ones. The fact that my family had been separated from me did not negate the happiness we had shared or steal those memories from me. I knew that.

What was more difficult was knowing how to adjust to life without them and not simply trying to relive the good memories, while still not forgetting them. I had to learn to focus on the future in place of the past. Because as much as I might want it, everything about those days was over. The family unit had come to an end for me. Even if, perhaps, I married again someday, I would never have children again. Not now. I would never be a mother again; I would never be a grandmother, no matter if the thought of grandchildren had just brought me joy. If I became a wife again someday, it would not be in the same way without the rest of the family as part of the household. And even that possible future felt very distant, as indeed it was: if it would ever come to pass, it would be years still before I would be ready for such a step. Until then, I would just be me, alone with only friends and no family.

Time was still difficult, whatever other answers I found. It was the dilemma of time that confused me. The gap of time that remained in my life after theirs ended caught in my steps and made me stumble. The gap of time that stood lonely and empty in my future made eventual joy seem so far and distant and unattainable to me. The gap of time clouded my breaths with dust and I didn't know, whatever else I was capable of, how I could defeat the gap of time. Choking dust was hard and physical and could not be avoided; the dust of shattering time would stand within my footsteps no matter what I did. I needed only to let my eyes, somehow, find some way to see past the dust that shredded my lungs and to look upon the bright sky that stood clear, outside of time. That was it. That was all and everything I had to learn how to do.

I reached out for the last rose once more, deciding that I wanted it near me, whatever else happened next. This time I took it by its base and gave it a tug. It hurt. It hurt as if the flower grew out of my own skin. But a breath of relief came with the pain as I placed the round rose in my palm and let its aroma rise to my nose. Thick and sweet, the scent closed my eyelids with its embrace. I felt my head lifting toward the sky in a prayer for grace.

One rose in a thorny world, echoing the words of the sky.

Maybe it wasn't so bad. I kept telling myself that I didn't want to be here, that I wanted to be home again, but this walk was rather nice, if I tried not to think of where I'd rather be. If I did, then each step I took was like forcing my foot onto hot coals. That was, I admitted, quite understandable. I couldn't expect to enjoy being here if my thoughts were elsewhere.

So I set aside my thoughts and just let myself breathe, accepting oxygen into my lungs to fuel the movement of my body. By this process, the hot coals cooled and I felt instead a necessity for speed, for setting my steps down again and again on the rough path. My very existence seemed to require this new focus for its concentration; my head and my thoughts would not survive without it. The connections between my mind, lungs, and feet began to work inside me in a circling cycle of motion. By molding together, their strength multiplied and I was able to think without being burdened by discontent, which was an amazingly strong force.

I found myself eyeing my uncomfortable surroundings once again: my distraction of rapid walking had unexpectedly brought my thoughts back to my location. It was maybe true that even if this wasn't my favorite place to be in, it was an interesting subject for contemplation. It was so strange to me, this place. It was a place of water, water in its every form, like an exploration of water. There was misty water in the air, which ought to be dry the way I had always known it; otherwise how could people breathe? There was even a wide body of liquid water to my right, as opposed to the cactus-covered hills that I loved; there was more water in that unending pool than anyone could ever drink. Yet the sun here was gentle rather than harsh, thus easing my afternoon walk. I accepted that as an improvement.

There were trees here, as well. They reached bold and broad against the water's background. Funny things I found them, sculpted at odd angles that often reached out toward the water and growing leaves like feathers on their upper arms. All followed the same pattern of form except for one. The tree's color, I noticed, was also off. I was drawn to this single change in scenery and began speed walking even more as I considered the singularity of the tree's appearance. Standing closer, I saw that it was a black tree. I didn't understand why it differed from the rest, so I examined it more closely.

Its base was cone-shaped. Upwardly it curved, dancing away with a wind that was not there. Yet only a very strong wind would be able to move that darkness of a tree; as great as the illusion of motion was, it remained but an illusion. One of the tree's arms, the lowest one, stretched horizontally, crossing the air with adamant and a very humanlike grace for all the straightness of the angle. A bit of limb, a nose to smell out the air, stuck out in the opposite direction. Branches began too quickly, not allowing me to see as much of the curving trunk as I wanted. The branches stuck upward like grasses in a bundle. Then they strained away, each in its own particular pattern. They had the same veined look as lighting, though they were more elegant. Little needles of black ice pierced out at intervals. Chaotic sensors these were, or else I knew not what. But the skin of this tree was intriguing. I saw smooth gray working across it, mostly on the trunk. Gray patches faded into flat black at the highest points. Golden black water spread behind the tree, colored perhaps by the shadow of its gaze; the horizon was honey-colored and the sky a dark topaz to match the water.

Such an odd tree. So great was its strangeness that it hurt me to look at it, yet I could not help but to look, to stare, even. Maybe I just I couldn't keep up with the thoughts and preferences of my mind anymore, even with my distractions. It was a dense muddle of confusion, burning me with each turn it made. So many things, feelings, there were, but I could no longer focus on only one of them or understand what they all meant or even take charge over them. It was easier to just close the control room in my mind and let the liquid thoughts flow through. This way I barely recognized their individuality, letting a single acute current of emotion thrill through my lungs. They grew excited at the pretense of life, breathing in a deep bit of air, pausing for a moment, then letting the air back out more slowly when my mind began to catch up with Thought.

This way of breathing and thinking was not torture, despite its strangeness, because I felt as though living in this way made me at least partially in control of myself. Yet neither was it pleasure. I was pressed against so hard by all of my errant thoughts that I forgot why to be joyful, as I had been not so long ago in my old home, in a place where I'd felt safe. That simple time was gone.

I wanted to give myself now to this intensity of thought I'd discovered, to succumb to its grasp on me, so that perhaps through it I could find comfort again. But all was confusion: thick, immense branches. They intertwined with one another in aching confusion. A black tree. Yet this tree, for all that it seemed a patch of darkness past understanding, fascinated me. It would not let me go. So I did all that I could think to do: I clung to it in return. I let the delirium seize me day after day that I came here, bowing my back under the pain that came from staring at it for so long, yet delighting in such a strong bond.

IX.II

Abigail fled without speaking to anyone or waiting for the scouts to arrive. She stepped away from the crowd to watch the morning in silence, to try and forget, for a moment, what she did not want to know. If she delayed receiving confirmation for what she had seen, then perhaps the universe would have time to imagine a new explanation for what her eyes knew was true. The empty air, at least, would help her feel less of a shock: she couldn't receive the news just now, so soon after waking. Her half sleeping mind was too fragile already, and it did not help that she had been dreaming of death. To hear that her dreams were real would overcome her; her eyes would close once more and she would never want to open them again. She could not be so publicly weak as that. So she fled away from all echoes of the reality of dreams, seeking instead, just for a moment, the reality of a still morning of ivory sky and sunlight blooming across a sleeping world.

Although she expected to be alone, Abigail found herself standing next to an old woman wrapped in a thin, knitted shawl.

Though small from age, the woman was otherwise not terribly distinguishable; Abigail recognized her by the shawl that she always seemed to be wearing, whatever the weather. She had not, however, spoken much to her before and knew little about who she was or how long she had been traveling with the group. After all, Abigail had not been part of this group long enough to learn everyone's story, and everyone here had a story; some of them were quicker to tell their stories, while others were content with letting the past stay quiet. All of them were here because they were fleeing from Them, and the flight had been perilous for many. Abigail wondered how well the woman had known Grey, or if she even knew yet that the men had just returned without him. If she had not seen them herself, which was probably the case, then Abigail could not be the one to tell her such news. If Abigail could not tell this reality to herself, then she could even less easily give the message to another person.

The woman beckoned Abigail to sit beside her; together they looked out at the land, as though leisure and enjoyment were all that mattered in their lives. For just one moment, loving to look upon the land really was all that mattered; they were so separate here from everything else. Abigail felt still, watching the yellow sun bleed across the sky's dome. Slowly the gray shadows came into more focus and all the life came into view. Where the two women sat was a pale, rounded rock among many similar boulders; the scattered arrangement of stones was like a circular camp. But around them stood quiet hills with less boulders and only gentle shrubbery. Compared with most of the other places where they had been, this space was defined by shades of darker green, at once more bold and more calm. They were closer here to northern regions; here was where the cactus met with the pine and the two comingled. The look of these two plants dwelling together gave the landscape a specific look, which infused hope within Abigail, as long as she tried not to see the image of the five figures walking into the morning. By blood the sun had risen before her eyes for too long; she couldn't bear to awaken to yet another stolen sunrise of darkness.

"Stop and listen to the breath," the woman said. "As the breeze floats by, the desert dryad's breath waves across your skin. Do you feel her breathing?" Her voice was soft, and though there was something serious in it, Abigail couldn't tell whether or not she meant to describe a literal story. Maybe she was referencing some figure of myth or fantasy.

"Who is she?" Abigail didn't know what else to say, until she realized that she was not meant to say anything, only to listen. Listening was easier than trying to answer, though Abigail still did not understand what the woman meant by these words. That made her feel like a poor listener. The woman continued speaking, either because she was oblivious to Abigail's confusion or because it did not matter to her whether or not Abigail understood her words.

"Do you see her hair in the clouds? Her skin is in the sandy dirt and her heart in the clay. Her feet walk with the brush, her fingers move with the cactus." With each reference, the woman's eyes moved all across the land as if pointing to everything that she mentioned.

"The mountains are her limbs, reaching up toward her father the sky. The sun is her mirror, making her to shine and gleam like gold in the eyes of anyone who believes enough to see her." Gently, she turned to face Abigail with a questioning gaze, though once again Abigail could tell that no answer was expected of her.

"Do you see her? Do you feel her?" Then the woman's gaze went back to the land and the brightening sky dome.

"Just a breath, and she's there. Treading toward the sky."

The woman smiled and clasped Abigail's hand. Then she rose and walked away, back toward the main group. Abigail felt like she was missing something, one last piece of information that could make the picture hopeful or tragic. She had to ask one more question.

"But wait," Abigail called after the woman, "if her bones are in the land, is she death or is she life?"

The woman turned around to face her again. "She can be both. She's you. So the choice is yours." Then she kept walking, leaving Abigail alone to ponder.

IX.III

Two decades ago, Nathan and I had driven to Camp Verde together, stopping at the historic Clear Creek Church on a bright Thanksgiving Day. We didn't care that we were breaking tradition by traveling together: if we were to leave together, why not also arrive together? Besides, I found that I cared very little for most wedding traditions, venue included. Some of my friends might have expected me to choose one of the beautiful resorts in the state or perhaps, if I wanted a striking outdoor wedding, somewhere in Sedona. Yet I had chosen this smaller location instead. I was happy with this place because I found this place beautiful: it suited my plan for a unique wedding. There was stillness here and simplicity, and these promised to me a more realistic idea of happiness than grand places with false and temporary ideas of perfection that had nothing to do with individuals and their daily lives; here, I had thought, was a reality that would last.

The church building, which had later become a school for about thirty years, was no longer in operation as either; instead, it waited quietly for visitors who came by to see the outside of the historical building. On the occasional day, like this day, wedding attendees were the ones who came. The church was a small structure made of large, limestone bricks as pale as the surrounding area's white dirt. Each roughly hewn stone was textured in colors of cream and peach and felt rough and smooth as sand. The grout in between was like tan cement framing each brick. There were six long, vertical windows on either side of the church and a gray, pitched roof overhead. A chimney and a wooden bell tower with a small cross on top stood on the front portion of the building; everything was traditional in design, though all of it was also singular in its loveliness. A pine tree, around the same height and width as the building, grew on one side; only the eccentricity of the tree's wide shape made me forgive it for almost completely blocking the view of the church from the street. Even if I wished for more openness, I was rather fond of the tree.

The truth was, I liked the placement of the church as much as the building itself. The way that the stone structure sat in an open clearing, surrounded by fluffy mesquite trees, gave the overall feel that we were up on the sky's altar. Here we climbed above all the rest of the world and the air we breathed in had a touch of clarity from being up so high. The white stones beside us were like the clouds, and we were in the very midst of the atmosphere. As I looked around, I couldn't imagine having chosen an enclosed, completely indoor location: layers of walls and closed doors would have given no sublimity.

I set my feet onto the cement path leading to the honey-colored, wooden door. Layers of lace gathered at my waist before falling down in a long skirt. The Victorian cut bodice had a row of buttons in the front and lacing in the back; it was not, however, pulled tight in true Victorian style. A V-shaped neckline led into three-quarter length sleeves edged in lace that rested at an angle. The lace on the main sections of the dress was different from the kind on the sleeves: it was sheer and cream-colored and held a pattern of delicate flowers. I was the only one amused by the fact that the dress was inspired by the 1880's, while the church had not been built until the turn of the century. In my mind, the two eras ought to have matched to add more cohesion to the wedding pictures. But I did not so much favor the 1900 dress silhouette and no one else thought that it mattered, so the difference in time remained. My hair I let flow in rustic curls down my back, mostly covered by the veil. My hands held the stems of purple lavender mixed in with various other flowers of muted colors, including pale pink roses.

Our ceremony was small; our guests were few. And nothing was there to distract me from why I was here. I had only one hope, and it was strong.

I remembered looking at Nathan's face; the sky outlined it and the sun lit it. When I walked down the path with him on our way out of the church, it was like proof that the world could hold perfection. Hands united, we were the entire world, filling in my vision up on this place. I looked at him and saw myself in his eyes and knew that he, too, found himself in me. I smiled, closed my eyes, and lifted my face up to the gentle sun in my thanksgiving. That day had been happiness.

Every Thanksgiving since, the celebration of joy and family had become even more grand. It was the single day when the nation deliberately chose to forego negativity in favor of peace and community, and it was the single day that stood, at once, for everything Nathan and I loved. It was the day of family, of looking together brightly on the past and setting up our hope for the future. And then it also became the day of us. Instead of separating the two celebrations, we blended them. We would arrange our wedding picture in its wooden frame near the middle of our holiday display of pumpkins and cornucopias. Sometimes we hid gifts for each other among the dinner table's dishes; I would set a gift box behind the breadbasket or Nathan would secretly set a box of truffles on my plate. One year I was tempted, just to be crazy, to hide a present inside the turkey for him to find while carving, but settled for the folds of his cloth napkin instead. When she was eight, Charlotte had glued our faces on the pinecone turkeys she had made, complete with wedding attire, and placed the two of them in front of our picture. I still had those turkeys and, tattered as they might become with age, I couldn't imagine how I could ever get rid of them.

People had teased us, calling us smart for getting married on a holiday so that we would always remember our anniversary, though in fact the exact date usually didn't match up with Thanksgiving Day. They also wondered why we had chosen such a public day, a day designed for big family gatherings and not for one-on-one time. They wondered why we didn't want the day of our anniversary to be ours alone, or at least why we always celebrated the two days together. Quite simply, though, I had always loved Thanksgiving and the idea of sharing the day I loved with the person I loved most was irresistible. Nathan, who was a child of the autumn, was glad for the fall setting of mild weather and clear sunlight, with trees and other plants slipping into winter's dormancy. Instead of thinking of it as the season of sleep, Nathan had called it the time of regeneration. As our wedding approached, he had pretended that he was taking me camping for the honeymoon to take advantage of the fall weather.

Knowing full well that we had made other plans and he was only teasing me, I told him that camping would be fine for the six-month anniversary.

When we were first married, I used to dream about him in the colors of November, of the brown suit he wore for the ceremony, of the soft gray in his eyes. I saw leaves falling and I thought of him, of how we had walked across fallen leaves on our wedding day. Cooling weather reminded me of warming hearts and I never felt a chill all through winter, knowing that the quiet time was a time for absorbing love and strength in order to start another year. When spring came, sometimes I still wore brown and tan instead of pale green and white: I wanted to hold on to the November of Nathan for as long as I could. I had so loved the season and the man.

When Nathan's autumn came to have a new meaning, one of loss and emptiness, all of my symbols changed. As the warmth of fall faded into my cold and lonely winter, I lost my sense of colors. Brown and grey were no longer magical shades, and fallen leaves screamed out to me beneath my feet in the agony of death. I couldn't wear color and yet I hated to see color fade from the land, and even wearing neutral tones made me sad, leaving me comfortable in nothing but the black reserved for grief. Thanksgiving, spent with Jesse and Sharon's family, was not the same. Though everyone was kind, they were not my family and I did not even know most of them. The way they all heartily greeted me like a lost child made me feel like a lost child, and all of the richness was gone. This day, into which I had once infused everything, had been emptied of so much that it now felt hollow. There seemed to be nothing left in a day that was just a name with no more meaning anymore.

That day, years ago, that we had spent together, that day had been happiness. Maybe I had misread the place of happiness.

X.I

I think maybe I was dead. Rushing and screaming, my mind was pulsing through strands I couldn't stop to hold onto. No focus came to me; nothing paused even for a moment. I walked but I thought that I must have been falling; there was no way that my mind could be supporting itself right now. Or was it my body that had to support my mind? The body controlled the tangible, but was the mind tangible or intangible? Did it rely on the body or hold itself separate? The mind and the body. Were they at constant war or constant harmony? Given how agonized I felt because of them both, I was leaning toward the former. Such chaos could only result from war, not from harmony; I felt no harmony right now.

The mind or the body. Where the role of one ends and the other begins is impossible to say. They are in such a tight battle within you that distinguishing between them grows meaningless and one word, one name, is not any different from the other. They circle endlessly around each other, fading in and out of dominance over your being. They both rule you until you do not know where you are or who you are. You only know that you are being ruled, controlled past your will; your will is nothing but something forgotten, vanished and murdered with time. My mind had fallen in the struggle long ago and had twisted around into a rusted coil, so now my body also was dead to reality within the coil of my mind. The two beaten beings, the mind and the body, glared at each other from the ground, wondering which would win in weakness in the end. Who won made no difference to me, when it was my life that was lost either way.

I walked on, but the movement meant nothing when I was reeling inside. My mind covered up any of the beauty of nature that might have been here and concealed from my body the healing effects of walking. My own confusion took over the landscape and as I walked, I imprinted myself into every curve of the path and every wisp of cloud that tore across the world. They were there, I became convinced, to express my pain and to torment me with every possible thing I had done wrong. I was not good enough for this place, and I made everywhere I went worse. That was what my wonderful mind told me.

The aching realization of necessary action burned as a hot coal in my belly, filling me entirely so that I could consume nothing else. It made me nauseous, and it made my head unsteady on my shoulders. I knew the hot coal was there. I knew it was the pain of all that I was not doing, all that I should be doing. I knew it was there, and I felt it like a round and unmoving and much too solid mass with each step that I took, but I didn't yet have the power to discern its meaning or its message. It just confused me. I didn't know what it wanted from me. It didn't give me any details, only guilt. No words, only pain. My body cried out at the sting of its bitter heat, and my mind retracted away from the riddle of the enigma of the hot coal within me. I was burning from the inside, all through to the outside, burning with the pain of a flameless round fire that I feared would never go out.

I think maybe I was dead. Screeching and halting halfway between a scream out of the depths and a fall down into a canyon,

I withered with nowhere else to turn. I withered like the dead

leaves of a once living tree, fallen prey to the trials of the wind

and the clouds and the beating of time's blackened heart. Life

promises everything, and time takes it all away. I twisted. I

twisted far away from everything I had ever held onto, and I

warped into something I no longer recognized. I warped into a

thousand shapes based on a thousand images thought of by my

mind and my body in a moment of delirium. And I said, let the

delirium seize me. Let it come. If I can't walk away from it, let it

come. What love do I have of rationality, anyway?

X.II

They said that they would burn flowers as a tribute to

him. There could be no burial because they had no body to bury,

which was a fact Abigail did not want to dwell on, but at least

they could honor him in this way. The passing of his life

deserved some kind of marker. So the group gathered together at

the meeting of two tall stones near where Abigail had spoken to the woman with the shawl that morning. Here they fell into a line to leave to rest their wildflower findings, which they had picked throughout the day; it was now already late afternoon. Abigail lingered toward the edges of the crowd, letting them all go ahead of her. This ceremony itself was already too much; she couldn't bear to look at the flower pile while it was still small and not at all noteworthy. She waited until it was heaping with the love of companionship, as represented by a plentiful assortment of flower-gifts.

Others could not bear to see the pile at all. Grey had been a friend to each one of them, it seemed, now that he was gone, and for some a ceremony only amplified his loss. It was a solidification of the news of his death. Therefore, by the time Abigail came to the pile of flowers, someone had already touched it with flame, willing the funereal time to end quickly. And yet to Abigail the burning of the petals was the worst image.

The wildflowers had been sweet when she picked them from the ground in mingled tenderness and anger; now they turned to bitter dust. So quickly the fire spread and ate the thin stems and sheer petals, one and then another and then all of them. Why did the light, the flame, have to rain ashes down on this miserable world of the earth? Couldn't it just come to them in its own glowing form, like the light from the sun and the stars? Brightness was a joy, but wasn't fire death? The flowers would bloom no more; their color was gone forever and soon nothing would be left of them. The light had taken them far away from the scope of the world.

Oh, Grey, Abigail said silently, you saved my life; I sent yours down to the depths. A pile of burnt flowers! Even more souls to lose their lives. Even more flame to burn across the beauty of the earth. Why did we think that would be a tribute?

"Abigail."

"Don't." She didn't want to hear their voices, all tinged in pain, drenched in tears no one would shed but that still drowned each of their throats. It was crude to speak so. Silence ought to be their only friend now. Silence was the only one whose attention she wanted, except perhaps for stillness. She did not want to speak and she did not want to leave this place, not yet.

The hand that went with the voice took her arm gently, steering her away. There was nothing more to do; the rocks only partially concealed them from any scouts who might be in the area. Though the smoke had never been voluminous and was already gone, anything out of place could arouse suspicion out here, and their loss was making everyone more worried than usual. Their task of remembrance done, everyone except Abigail wanted to leave as soon as possible. No precaution felt too much. In any case, Abigail had no more reason to mourn than anyone else, and so she started away from the flower pile. If the others found the strength, outwardly at least, to go on, then so must she. She had no more claim to Grey than any of them did and no more reason to grieve.

Her skirt brushed the gray ashes of the dead flowers as she walked by. It made her feel unclean, as if she had just taken part in murder. Grey's murder. He was one with the flowers and the nature of this land. They were innocent and comforting; blameless and calming. An eternal presence of safety and kindness. But she had sent him away from them all through selfish desire of a selfless person's goodwill. Not just a murder but a betrayal: all the while, he had called her one of the good people. But if not for her, Grey would not have lost Alice and would not have felt the need, out of grief, to be part of the forays away from the main group. He would have stayed to fulfill his role as the leader of the whole, not escaped into one small part of it. She knew that he would have stayed where it was safer: he, of all of them, had needed to stay alive to help them. But now that he was dead, he showed himself as a mere man; he had not saved them.

Abigail led the hand and the voice to the other side of the rocks. They were Grey's headstones now; in their faces, Abigail hoped to see his and to remember why he had so persevered in life, what it was he had held onto when he was strongest and had wanted her to hold onto, too. No one believed it healthy for her, or indeed for anyone, to be alone right now, hence her audience; they were trying to take care of each other, of even her. Yet perhaps it was better this way, better that she didn't condemn herself to silence; someone to talk to might remind her that, somewhere, life still existed. His presence also forced Abigail to maintain some sort of confidence, however weak: she didn't want to crumble if she was being watched.

It made her at least approach the place with hope. If a headstone completed everyone's life, then she decided that at least this one was pleasant. The rocks were like the fingernails of the earth; they were little bits of shine on the hand it stretched out to the sky. Grey was a part now of this movement out towards the breath of the sun. He had the tip of the land to stand with him and to protect him. It was a comforting concept, except . . . did in fact such a security within the land exist? If everything else was immaterial and temporary, then why not this?

"What if the land dies? This tissue is dead. The shape of a skull I see lurking in the mixed colors of that rock's face, its eyes pierce out at me. I see Alice's nurturing smile in one empty socket and Grey's unfaltering visage in the other. There is no chin, rather a wide space of a mouth in blackness that waits to inhale what life here in us remains." As Abigail spoke, her words grew more haunted and her eyes began to pulse against their sockets.

"I see it. He's pale." The voice offered her no comfort, and neither did she want any: she needed only to speak now, to speak such fears as she had never felt before. Everything that once had been solid trembled and she feared for her very bones. She was uncertain if there was any stability anymore.

"What if the land dies? If the tissue dies, why not the land? The tissue felt real, was accepted as real every day that it lived. If it did not endure, then how can the land?

"What if the land dies? Would it sigh a breath of death? Would the trees flail about one last time and the mountains lose their healthy pallor? And would the wind wheeze and cough? The red cave mouths open and close with last words that no one would understand?"

She had relied before on the land, thinking it the most natural and eternal part of her world. She had relied on Grey, thinking him the best person she knew. But if all betrayed her, whom then could Abigail trust? She could trust no one in this mortal world and died today to life.

X.III

All through the holiday season, I felt heavy. All through this holy time, I missed the joy I used to always have here at the end of the year, remembering the early days of our marriage. Of all the year, this had been the best time. So now it was the worst time. Where before my sorrow had been able to pass unnoticed, now it grew more difficult to mask it. The sorrow also grew. But I did try to not let it have its way. I kept occupied by day; I ran the store from opening to closing, even on weekends. At least Carol never had to worry about asking me for time off when she wanted it: I was always at the store, whether or not I needed to be. I wrapped up the vintage glass and plastic ornaments people had purchased and gave the occasional opinion on potential gifts; it was a cheery atmosphere. But by night, I dwelt at home and had to close my eyes to the glitter of the house's usual Christmas lights. Because the street was always so celebratory for holidays, setting out piles of decorations and grand displays, I could not pass on lights this year, much as I might want to; I cared about this community too much to let mine be the only dark house. But I could also not grow excited over the lights. So much red and green and white, all lit up with a yellow glow, only reminded me of why I was sad. Red the color of love became the color of pain, and the bliss and verdancy of green grew into the corruption of rotted life. As for white, all of its purity faded away into the starless sky of death. I felt so heavy.

The daylight faded into dark so early these days that I thought I must not be the only one tired and drained. Early evenings felt like early endings to the working days, even if the time on the clock said differently. Coming home one evening, I fell on the nearest sofa to the door and found sleep without even asking for it. It was only an hour or two later that I lifted up my eyes, not because I was rested enough but because I wanted to raise myself out of a dream. It was not a bad dream, but it might as well have been.

In the dream, I saw the image of a face. It was not a face I had seen in person in years, but it was one I knew well: it was the face of our daughter as a baby. That was a face so dear to me that I would never forget it. When I had first held each of my children in my arms, I had vowed to protect them. The loss of Andrew five years after Charlotte was born made me feel that I had failed him, and I had vowed every day after that I would not also fail Charlotte; I would not let my promise to her also disappear into nothing. Looking in her soft and new face when she was born, I had thought that the world could not help but to keep her safe with me forever, that my task would be easy. I thought once, so long ago, that life would be spared for the sake of sweetness. Now I saw that small visage once again within my eyes, and now my misconceptions were gone.

I couldn't stand to look at her face.

Not because she wasn't pretty. Not because she wasn't happy. Not because I had done anything wrong to her. Despite all that I still struggled with, I had, at least, moved beyond the feeling of guilt. I knew none of this was my fault; that was not why I retreated. So many comingled emotions fell over me when I looked into that perfect face that I simply had to jerk myself away. I felt insignificant when I looked at her. I felt so far away from her perfect childhood innocence, something I had been so far away from for so long. Why, I was practically jealous of my once daughter.

But no, it was not really jealousy of her. I couldn't be jealous of my own daughter, even of a dream of her. It was jealousy of the life I had lost. It was jealousy of perfection. It was the wish that I could have had another kind of existence, the life that had so abruptly been interrupted. I had wanted that life so much, and I had planned for it for years. I had not lost the nuclear family because of divorce or custody issues or a desire for independence or any of the thousand other reasons that a solid unit of four rarely existed anymore. I had been so close to it that I had held it within my grasp and then lost it through no cause of my own. I didn't know how I could recover from losing everything. But he and she were gone, and I tried to shake off their lingering impression while I forced myself to stand up.

Even my body was sore, which was, however, a natural result from sleeping on the small sofa. The fabric held little cushioning and I fit very barely within its frame; it was an old sofa designed for sitting up straight on the edge, not for lounging. Probably I was mad for letting myself fall asleep on it at all, but it had seemed the closest piece of furniture when I had come inside. I hadn't thought ahead; I had just fallen apart wherever I could. The leather sofa would have been better for a rest, or even my bed upstairs. Then I might have actually found some peaceful rest, away from dreams of my past.

A bout of grumpiness passed through me as I walked up to my closet to change out of my work clothes. I knew that I was expected to live with that dreamed image beneath my lashes and yet to live with strength and joy, perhaps even all the more for the experience. Living through this was supposed to open my eyes to the reality of life and the world, letting me live with greater enrichment or some such something. But that concept did not sound very appealing right now and it certainly did not comfort me or make me feel enriched, so I regarded it with a certain measure of reluctance. Hearing about what I was supposed to feel or do did not help me; it only created new struggles within my mind, making me feel lost and behind.

I walked over to the kitchen a quarter of an hour later, slightly more composed and hoping for everything to straighten out. At least, I was quieter now, perhaps from the darkness of all the empty rooms; the sound of tears and protests echoing from empty rooms had shut my mouth. Standing at the counter, I held my hand out over a ceramic mug, dropping a tea bag inside its circle. I couldn't find the teakettle. I couldn't even remember how long it had been missing. So I set a small saucepan of water on the stove and waited for it to became vocal as the burner blew bubbles of steam into the water's surface. I watched for a moment the carelessness of the water. It broiled and bubbled as if such an intrusion of heat were only natural, as if it knew that the air would quickly cool its temper away. It was annoying water, really.

I poured it into my tea mug where it belonged.

I hoped that if tea was considered a comfort item, it could give comfort even to such as I. I would not find the solace I needed in trying to sort things out, so perhaps I would find it within this small comfort. The tea had nothing to do with all that troubled me, and maybe that was what I needed. Fitting my hand around the warm mug, I felt the heat from inside fade into my fingers. The tea bag hung from its white string on the surface, hovering as it lost its breath before sinking towards the bottom. As soon as the water turned dark, I tossed out the dead skin of the bag, bringing the mug finally to my lips and taking myself to the window seat in the living room.

This was one of the rooms I most hated being in by myself: here it was that he and I used to sit together, or where we used to be when company came over. Except for when I cleaned, I had never spent time here alone. It was our space, not mine. If I forced myself to come in right now to try and get over the feeling of dread, at least I would not sit on our leather sofa, glaring into the empty room. This was, probably, the same reason why I had gone to the narrow sofa to sleep on when I came home: I had not wanted to approach the memories of the brown leather, even if it was more comfortable. From my place at the window seat I could look out instead of just in. Situated on its cushions, I drank from the brew in my hand, trying to derive simplicity out of my surroundings. I tried to approach the truth as facts; facts I might be able to overcome.

So she was gone, as he had gone before. So he also was gone. So I was here. So the cup of tea remained fresh. So the house was still as wonderful as ever it had been and as much as ever I had wanted. So I was still alright, wasn't I? Still I was friends with Jesse and Sharon. Still I would work on my antique shop. Still people would come in and out of my life's path, right there for me to help or otherwise influence for good—or for them to influence me. Still I would keep on living as always I had. As far away as my family was, was I alone, even without them? Had all the colors really faded, and had all the symbols really changed? Surely some things remained the same.

I pulled out a book from the side table's drawer. The wood scraped softly and the book slid slightly from the movement. I let my fingertips linger on the binding as I drew open the pages, breathing in their scent of paper. The book I balanced on my knees, while my tea, pressed against my leg for balance, I held in my right hand. Both items were warm, and as the daylight outside my window faded completely into quiet night, I looked at my book's weathered cover and suspected I would get out of this mood eventually.

XI.I

As I approached the tree one day, I could see something marring the rough and regular surface of its body. The texture and color in one long section were not the same as the rest of the smooth, black bark. I left my usual path and walked right up to it; I needed to see what was on this tree that I passed by daily. If something had changed, I had to know; it might make a difference. Anything new might help me better understand the tree, or at least give me something else to focus on instead of monotony. Even a little change would be worth taking a closer look. What I found was not exactly as strange as I had expected, though it still made an impression on me.

A thick liquid felt its way down the length of the trunk, the amber across the black. I reached out my hand to feel the wound. I didn't know why, maybe because I wanted to see if it was real, but all I could think about was touching the amber liquid. My hand wanted to be there on the open bark, holding in the golden liquid instead of letting it keep flowing out. As I touched it, however, the blood stuck to my fingers. The sensation was strange and unpleasant: not only was the blood sticky, but it also felt half-hardened, as if, once on my skin, it would forever coat my fingertips. If it truly were becoming solid, then water would never wash it away; it would stay as an unwanted amber layer over my fingers, sealing my skin and blood. Such a feeling of permanent uncleanness as this begged my hand to move away, yet I could not loose my touch. I remained fixed, for a long moment, with my hand reaching out toward the split bark.

It was not that I felt sorry for the tree: wounded or not, its strength remained great, and it would be fine with any less injury than having its trunk cut down. In any case, a little running sap, at least, did it no harm, as much as the sap might flow away like blood. Sap was a normal sight on a tree. The tree felt no hurt from it, and I had not inflicted the wound, or broken the bark. But all the same, I felt responsible for hurting this tree that had taunted me. I didn't know why, but I felt guilty, as if there was something I had done wrong. Although I couldn't think of how to wipe the sap from my skin, removing it was the only thing on my mind now, just as the idea of touching it had been before. If the sap was a result of any kind of ill, or if even somewhere in my mind I thought that it might be, then I didn't want it on me. I didn't want to be a part of any of it. I wanted to run away from it all, away from every possible situation, and I didn't want this tree to keep following me. It was a frightening tree, making demands of me and forcing me into confusing reactions.

I tried to forget, or to ignore, that I had willingly reached out to touch the flowing sap and that I had wanted so much to touch the bark. I couldn't acknowledge that, not now that I fled the blackened tree, terrified of I knew not what. I couldn't admit that I was curious about the tree; I couldn't admit that if it were hurt, I would be sad. It just seemed wrong to fear the tree and then care about it, though I hardly knew why I should feel so strongly either way or why it should make a difference if I changed my opinion. What was one black tree in a world full of green trees? There couldn't be anything special about it. I was just making up false meaning and undeserved interest. This was all just another manifestation of my confusion, and I was wasting time with it. I tried to put it out of my mind.

XI.II

At least the camp was a busy place. It came complete, day and night, with distractions from Abigail's allotted length of grief. *Pretend it isn't true*, she told herself. For now, at least, that was the guideline Abigail followed. Did she have a choice? She had to continue with whatever life she had begun to build here. She had little right to mourn so long and so deeply for someone toward whom she had no kind of claim. People died every day, and no one could grieve for all the world. To guard against such sorrow, the bonds that humanity could rightfully hold onto were the bonds of family; family, in turn, was defined by blood or marriage or at least friendship as strong as family. Abigail and Grey fit into none of these, and for that she was sorry. It was not that Abigail wished she had had a different kind of relationship with Grey, simply that she wanted the world to accept what connection they had shared. Otherwise she felt guilty taking time to grieve for him as more than just the group's leader while everyone else tried to move on from his loss.

She and Grey were not, in any way, family: Abigail did not even have any family anymore. There had never been romance between them and there never would have been; that wasn't their relationship at all. And they had never had the chance to become friends, maybe would not even have been friends in a calm and peaceful world. For whatever reason, their paths had simply not gone in that direction, and there was nothing wrong with that. The stage of friendship they had bypassed in favor of a deeper connection born of survival. The will to survive against a threatening foe had required the will to love. Without love, there could be no survival. Without love, they would both be long dead in more ways than one: Grey would not have helped Abigail escape and they wouldn't have given each other hope. But love did not require family or romance or even friendship. It was complete in itself, and it felt loss just as strongly because it came with no distractions. In this way Abigail had loved Grey, and in this way she mourned him, though she was not mourning a friend, a brother, a husband, or any other acknowledged connection. They had been fellow prisoners, but was that the most they could claim? It did little to express the truth. So Abigail continued following the pattern of life, hiding the grief within her.

As another evening fell, Abigail walked back toward her corner of the camp. Tradition was for everyone to eat together and then to spread out once more as dusk settled in; this kept them close but still allowed for personal space. A few people lingered in the main group to talk or to plan, but everyone else went away to complete their own tasks and seek quieter company. Abigail sought the company of solitude. She did, however, keep her hands busy while she sat: even if her mind was numb, her hands could still work. As her fingers straightened lengths of thread and moved a needle through the bare patches of a blanket, Abigail found herself facing toward the rising moon.

The full circle glowed from out of the sky, near toward the horizon; it was colored in golden orange. Normally the silvery moon was sharp. That was what Abigail always expected. Yet this orange moon was soft and warm, deep in its color. A hazy circle of yellow-red light surrounded the moon and somehow it stayed vibrant and darkened at the same time. Its colorful echo of sunlight was a reminder that the sun still drifted through the atmosphere even when the daylight was darkened by night. Under a bright moon, night's obscurity was not fearful, at least not anymore fearful than the day: even the day was not all about safety, as Abigail well knew. The glowing moon's color faded as it drifted higher into the sky, as also the last shreds of daylight faded from the land and from Abigail's eyes. She gazed upon the moon and felt as if the night world was a place completely different from the day world. She felt herself drifting into the land of the stars.

For every shadowy plant that the moon lit, there was a shining star to match it in the sky, even if most of the stars weren't visible behind the bright moon's light. For every dark pathway on the land, a crooked line traced within the remaining constellations. Abigail blinked back and forth between the land

and sky until she gazed only on the stars and saw unknown depths within the deep blue and the white glitter. The blue was soft and still, an endless atmosphere of openness. The stars, because of how brilliantly they shone, looked harder than the sky in which they sat. Their silver color was not like the golden glow that had reflected off of the moon; their color was steadfast and unchanging and unforgiving. It was also enthralling.

Thus it was that as the glowing moon shed its warm hue to match the standard, silver color of the stars, Abigail could not wish away its shade of pale. She was glad to have seen the gorgeous and golden color that came only occasionally, only for a short time while the moon was still close to the horizon. But the white moon, full in its brilliance, was also beautiful. This was the moon taking the sun's light and turning it into something new. This was the beautiful and the terrible, black and white contrasts set into a single dome of a sky. As she put away her mending and stretched across the fabric of her bed, Abigail stared at the white moon and tried not to think of anything else. She could not, or the grief would swallow her and she would have no excuse for allowing it.

XI.III

I went about the task little by little. When a house went from three people to one, there was much to sort through and rearrange. It would have already been a lot of work even if it weren't such emotionally draining work, and the emotional side was what made the timeline continually stretch onward until I thought I would never be finished. I had packed and unpacked many times in my life, but this was nothing like preparing to move. This was the reverse: instead of preparing for the future, I was putting away the past. And the past was an enormous entity that protested my efforts to pack it up neatly. Taking down Charlotte's posters, for instance, was harder than I would have thought, considering that I had never exactly liked them to begin with; they represented her favorite things, not mine. Her movies, her shows, her music. Though it was almost new, I donated her iPod because I didn't need it and I couldn't think of trying to sell it. The thrift store also received a good helping of clothing and half-forgotten toys; these I couldn't justify keeping, save for one or two favorites I couldn't part with. I also kept her little wooden jewelry box and everything that was inside, just a pair of earrings, an old watch, two toy dogs, and a pin from school. These were her collected treasures.

I don't know what was more difficult, dropping off Nathan's clothing or coming home to the empty space in our shared closet. Parting with his things was a challenge that I always knew I would come across, but the empty space was blankness. People told you what it was like to grieve. Tears and sorrow and shock and anger were all to be expected. But what they didn't explain was how to fill in the blankness. I let the two empty rows in the closet haunt me for weeks because I didn't want to cover yet another memory of Nathan with myself. It seemed cruel, materialistic and unfeeling. Selfish.

But space is space, I told myself eventually. And material things do not replace the immaterial, which stands above everything else; trying to hold the material as sacred would not help me. So I finally admitted that I really could use the extra space. At least if I made some changes the empty rows wouldn't stare at me anymore. Hopefully. My sweaters would be more organized if I moved the jackets away from them to one of the empty rows. I shifted the hangers over two by two. Then my hands felt busy, and my worries fell to the side in favor of action. I grew interested in what I was doing, until I had rearranged almost all of the rows, keeping form and color carefully in mind instead of sorrow and loss. I was even pleased, once done, at how much better my things fit in the space with this new arrangement. After all, closets were never big enough.

It was late now: I had not started on my reorganizing until after dinner. So I stepped out of the closet, going to the right toward the bathroom to get ready for bed. I pushed open the bathroom door and flipped on the light switch inside before walking in: it was my habit not to walk into the still-dark space without first turning on a light. This time I was glad for my caution. A crawler was there smiling at me. It stood right on the threshold to the bathroom, facing outward; probably it had been just outside, rather than inside, the closed door, though the difference mattered little anymore. Both places were directly in my path. Familiar though this crawler's image was, still its appearance was singular enough to be shocking every time. About two inches in size, it was a clear tan color. Four legs stuck out on either side of an oval body that carried two pincers in front as hands. In the back was the flying tail, a pointed drop suspended on a long curve. It was a scorpion that I had nearly stepped on while simply moving through my bedroom, from the closet to the bathroom.

When I saw the crawler, a sharp breath of air ran halfway up my throat. I hated finding scorpions in the house. It felt wrong, worse than finding flies or even spiders; scorpions belonged in their own space outdoors, not here. I knew I had to deal with the bug, though, before it had a chance to sting me; it wasn't deadly and wasn't the very harmful kind, but still that was an experience I would much rather do without. Even a fire ant's sting I always tried to avoid. And all of this was not to mention the fact that I didn't want any sort of bug roaming my house, whether or not it could sting. But the difference here was that dealing with a bug that could sting meant that disposing of it equaled killing it, which equaled smashing it. And it was the smashing part that I hated most.

However I loathed it all, I needed a smashing object, quickly. A few steps away, just inside the still open closet, was a pair of sandals for the yard and balcony. I grabbed one and tossed it toward the scorpion. Because of my weak effort, the shoe missed, of course, and the scorpion spiked its tail in reaction, ready to defend itself. This should have been so easy, but all I had done was warn it that I was coming. That was pathetic. Now I really had to hurry before it ran, mad, and found my bare feet; it was because my feet were bare that I hadn't been able to simply step on the scorpion, though, honestly, the idea of stepping on it was even less appealing than hitting it. I knew that this time I would have to get closer if I wanted to actually succeed in smashing the critter. So with the second shoe, I went nearer and, trying not to think about it, struck the scorpion and finally killed it. I shuddered at the idea of its broken body beneath the clear plastic sandal. A live scorpion was bad enough; a dead one was disgusting.

Yet for all my weak shudders over killing it, this creature had made me fearful and angry by dwelling in my house. Out of all places to be, it had showed up in my bedroom, right beside my bathroom. How dare it come to bother me? That was why, despite my reluctance, I had to kill it. We two could not share the same space. The scorpion and I, we had not the same ways. In my house, it was nothing but an intruder and there was no way to be rid of it but by its death. Bugs, of whatever kind, didn't belong in my house, and killing them was the only solution. It was not a solution I delighted in, which only made it worse.

Growing up, I had always run to someone else for help, never wanting to do the smashing myself. Maybe it had been a large spider in the middle of my room, a bee on the window, or even a scorpion on my bed one time. During my married years, I had often had Nathan take care of such simple things; even as an adult, I hadn't wanted to bother with any of it if I didn't have to.

And now here I was, stuck doing everything myself again. I wasn't even used to taking care of a simple spider anymore, which was probably why there were a few more cobwebs on the ceiling than there ought to have been; it wasn't as if they were there because I had stopped cleaning the house.

I felt like I was in my twenties and in college all over again, except that I was nowhere near twenty anymore: that was the only time when I had lived alone. All the excuses I had made back then no longer worked, though, not even if I was the only one who knew about them. I couldn't get someone else to do the tasks I disliked because no one else was here. I couldn't avoid sweeping because I was busy: work only took up an average amount of my time, no more. I couldn't eat nothing but pasta or cereal for dinner just because I didn't know how to make anything else: I needed more varied food and more fresh food than that now. And I could not let myself lag or fail today with the excuse that there was a whole future ahead of me tomorrow: half of my future was already behind me. Nothing was the way it had been when I was in my twenties.

The whole scorpion business over, I folded back the bedspread, contemplating the empty mattress space. Underneath the blanket, I curled up into a small size so that I wouldn't bother the emptiness. I tried to think, to remember. Before we were married, had I even had a full-sized bed? Or had it always been a twin? I couldn't remember if I had ever bothered to get a bigger bed than my childhood one when I moved out of home for college; after all, I didn't have much money to spend at that time and my apartment probably hadn't been big enough to make even a twin look small. Either way, I wasn't used to sleeping with my limbs all splayed out across a wide space. Yet it seemed silly to get a smaller bed now, even a full-size. A master bedroom was supposed to have a big bed, and even if I made the bed smaller, then I would just be creating more empty space in the room. I would probably get used to having this one to myself, anyway.

I sighed and closed my eyes. Images of shirts and scorpions and sheets came first to my lids before I shooed away the images and thought instead of the approach of spring. There were still several cold weeks ahead and there was always so much wind here that the warmth often felt delayed in comparison to nearby regions, but the transition would be soon approaching. This year I didn't want to hold onto autumn; I needed the spring to come right now. As the flowers began to bloom in yellow and pink, in yards and across hillsides and on the edge of the road, perhaps I could leave the bulk of my pain behind with the winter. And yet what ought to have been a comforting notion was just a tiny bit terrifying.

XII.I

Broken. Listen to the way it tumbles off your tongue. So much movement for such a simple word, the soft vowel smashing into the harshest consonant. When the word ends, it brings with it a command of finality. There is no going back from brokenness. There is no pretending it never happened. When you reach this harsh word all felt in a long moment of time, you can think of nothing else and cannot remember what it was like before you broke. I'm not sure whether or not this is a bad thing. I do, however, know this much: to whatever end, I was at last breaking, and it was shocking. Everything I had ever tried to hold myself up with had turned weak and left me raw without any false sense of support. I saw a world I had never seen before, though it was nothing different from what I had always seen; it was just to me that everything looked different now. I broke because, after thinking for so long that I could stand, I finally fell.

Falling. It is when the gravity of the earth conquers the will of the body. The body is weak, after all. I fell; my whole body collapsed into the sand beneath me. My mind broke and my body fell with nothing to keep it standing. I ended up on my back. I found my knees bent and my head flat against the sand. I was facing straight toward the sky, but the glare from the clouds made it too bright to look at directly; I was more aware of the solid world beneath me. Individual grains of sand are soft against your fingertips, but a beach of them beneath you is hard, except where each grain moves about to fit the shape of your body. I did not find this conformity comforting. Instead I found both the sky and the earth equally frightening: one blinded me, and one tried to swallow me. In just one fall, the grains of sand reached up to ground me to a grave, moving out of place to clasp all of my limbs in their arms. I forgot about trying to get up on my own; I thought I was stuck here without hope, and the pressure of fear exploded into my eyes. Because I did not know a way out and could not see anything that would help, I wept.

Tears. They come from the middle of the chest and surge like blood through the lungs and throat and head. They fill the eyes like boiling foam above a pan; the heat builds in a rage until it can no longer be contained. Once it is kindled, it cannot be stopped. The boiling tears when they overflow are blood bleeding from a wound without any stitches or bandages. As with a wound, so much pain accompanies the traces of water that you begin to view them as the physical representation of your pain; sometimes, indeed, they are the only visible aspect of a pain that would otherwise have stayed hidden. They are the thing that forces attention to a problem you do not want to approach. My wet pain, falling from my eyes, drained down my skin and into the sand. Maybe it faded away into the dry grains, or maybe the sand had been waiting all along to feed off of my tears. Maybe the red tears flowed down until they reached the ocean, falling forever out and away. These tears of mine overwhelmed me, as tears do. They only stopped, I didn't know how much later, when my eyes began to hurt, to throb with too much moisture gathered and too much moisture lost.

Silence. It comes to you when you are not sure what you feel. My face shattered in moisture, my tears and my thoughts both stopped. If the fear and the pain were still there, they no longer felt the same. My silent eyes wavered across the landscape.

XII.II

Abigail waited until they made camp near another patch of wildflowers. She had decided to pick them this time for their beauty alone in atonement for the flowers burnt at the funeral. Ever since that day, flower ashes had haunted her with a sorrow that flowed along like memory, silently wavering and nearly intangible. The old woman with the shawl stayed to help her while the rest of the group scattered to go about their own tasks; sometimes it did seem that the two of them were the least busy of everyone. While the other woman had age to keep her from working as hard, Abigail usually tried to keep up and do her part. But right now she needed this free moment. And, she told herself, it was only one afternoon that she was taking off; tomorrow she could fall back into the pattern of work. The fading footsteps of the distant crowd soon gave way to the silence of the two pairs of arms moving forward and back to pluck the yellow and orange flowers from the ground.

The old woman's name was Sylvia. She was slightly taller than Abigail and wore her pale hair with the top half held back by a cord of leather to keep the strands out of her way. Her eyes were black and her shawl a light brown material untouched by dye. She was Abigail's first friend here. Since their conversation on that nightmare morning, Abigail had come to learn more about this woman with the kind words. Sylvia was the last of her family: she had never married and had outlived all of her other relations; she said she had been with this group for a very long time, almost since its first days. She also told Abigail that they could become each other's family now; she believed everyone needed someone to look out for. So Abigail pictured Sylvia as Alice's oldest aunt, an image of the younger woman separated only by the passage of time, and at once felt comforted by the connection.

Even now, Sylvia's presence changed things. Abigail had begun picking the flowers out of lonely pain and if she had been alone, she might have only grown more sorrowful. Then she wouldn't have found hope from the task, only reminders of what she had lost. But with someone by her side, there was some joy left and her action ended like a casual, leisurely afternoon spent between friends. The two women then sat on the edge of the flower patch with their findings. They arranged the flowers by size and admired the best ones and let the sun sink into their limbs while they rested. Together, so many flowers could have made a spring bouquet—if there had been any desire for a bouquet out here.

Abigail picked up one of the yellow blooms and held it near her eyes. Within the single flower, the petals were like a bouquet of their own, one that had been carefully gathered and lovingly maintained. The bouquet was held together tightly, but also precariously: the petals could fall apart so easily under any disturbance. Time, as well, would make them to fall away without hesitation. They were more delicate than the roses and other flowers that grew in city gardens. Though they had the power to spring up on their own in the wilderness, these flowers wilted so quickly.

The only way, then, to possibly preserve the wildflower petals was to dry them at once. That was Abigail's plan. She only hoped that the camp's constant movement from place to place would not disturb the drying process. She had always dried other flowers by hanging them upside down, but that would not work when she was on the move like this. Maybe it wouldn't even work on this type of flower at all: they would lose all shape and color until they bore no resemblance at all to their previous faces. Because Abigail was not sure what materials she could use to dry the flowers by pressing, which seemed like the only drying option she had, Sylvia gave her two pieces of thick leather in place of the heavy books or stones people usually used. They arranged the flowers between the leather pieces and bound it all shut with a ribbon stretched several times across both length and width. There were no more available materials than these, yet it was all sufficient to give the flower petal bouquet a home.

"Will they survive?" Abigail asked her friend. She pictured the flowers turning to dust between their leather sheets.

"Maybe. Wildflowers do not lend themselves to drying. They will not look exactly the same as they do now. But if you are careful about the bundle, then I think you will be able to preserve some of their essence. Just enough to let beauty overcome ashes." Sylvia seemed to understand why the flowers had haunted Abigail; that in itself helped soothe her fears.

"They are very beautiful, the wildflowers," Abigail said. "So many of them grow here, all on their own. So much color, springing up toward the sun. The flowers come up every year without anyone calling for them. They do make me almost think I'm happy, just to see them again. It's this time of year, isn't it, that feels that way?"

"Spring is awakening the land. The time of sleep is ending, for all things. The flowers are rising. The snakes are emerging. The sun is lengthening its days. Like all of these, we also must wake up. Morning must come, or else the night was a waste and its time of rest accomplished nothing. Abigail, do not let yourself sleep overlong in sorrow."

To that Abigail gave no answer.

XII.III

Sharon was bringing her jewelry to a craft fair in Flagstaff; she made wrought iron necklaces, earrings, and bracelets, which I had always thought were a wonderfully tough take on feminine accessories. Though she went to more events in Prescott than anywhere else, she did go to Flagstaff from time to time. Jesse invited me to come along for the car ride, saying that we could use the opportunity for another hike while Sharon was at the craft fair. After helping Sharon set up her booth, the two of us drove to Sunset Crater. The site of the volcano was one of my favorite places to visit, so perhaps I would feel some measure of healing there. Jesse probably hoped so, as well, and had invited me for that very reason, making up an excuse about how the three of us could all have dinner together at the end of the day. But we didn't need to drive out of town just for dinner. If it hadn't been for me, Jesse would have either stayed with Sharon at the craft fair or let her go to Flagstaff on her own. I accepted his offer, though: I knew I needed a good day out after my long hours at the store all winter. The Prescott trail had been nice, but it had also been a while ago now, and I hadn't really gone anywhere since. I'd used the excuse that it was too cold in winter to be outside. Sometimes that was true—but it was also true that some places were better to visit in winter than summer, a fact that I had deliberately ignored.

Flagstaff was an hour and a half north of Prescott. The weather was cooler, and there were even more pine trees growing. It snowed much more here, leaving the summers milder than they were in Prescott. The extra difference made Flagstaff look like a completely different region from the Phoenix area, but that was simply the difference between the Northern and Southern halves of Arizona. The state covered a wide area, so it was only natural for the terrain to change many times from one end to the other. Here the land was quiet and calm, colored in blue and brown and green. It felt both older and younger than Prescott: the two cities had some shared history, but otherwise seemed to have followed very different stories. This place, Flagstaff, was also volcano territory, and it was with the volcanoes, not the handful of historical buildings, that I felt the territory's oldest roots.

Sunset Crater Volcano National Monument was past the town, a few minutes' drive around the tall San Francisco Peaks, which were also the remains of a volcano. Once you took the exit to the park, a long road made a half circle against the highway; Sunset Crater was in the bottom half and Wupatki National Monument was in the top half, though admission was considered the same to both places. Though Wupatki was the main pueblo, there were also others in the park. They were beautiful to look at, and while some were very much in ruins, other stood still mostly intact. Because Sunset Crater and Wupatki were essentially the same park, it was simple to see them both on the same day: you started at either end of the half circle road and returned to the highway on the other side without having to backtrack. Jesse and

I, however, were not planning on visiting the pueblos today: it was a fairly long drive to get to them from the Sunset Crater side and we were already doing enough driving today. We did, however, drive partially up the road simply to see the views: I would have thought it a shame not to go at least a short way. These views were part of what I loved about coming here.

Driving through the bare road, I looked to the sides of the car to see red and black comingled, the colors of the dirt. Because we were so close to the Painted Desert here, the earth was naturally colorful. The colors of the Painted Desert ranged from red and pink and yellow to white, blue, and purple; despite the stark emptiness of that region's landscape, there was more variety there than anywhere I knew. That land of enchantment, built by nature's art and beauty to a completely unique aesthetic, was just visible on the horizon. From here, it stood in shades of pink that made it echo a sunset on the edge of the land. It was like a dream, something so soft and beautiful it couldn't be real.

But the land's warmth here where we were was mixed with lost volcanic rocks, which brought the color of blackness to become part of the landscape. That made for a rather different effect, although not a bad one: I did also love these colors. Yet I could never tell if the land looked lost and lonely or simply rugged and wondrous; I watched so closely, as if the answer might suddenly become clear. Maybe it was all the contrast that made me hesitate to describe the mood. The red against the black. The stretches of empty land and the thick forests of pine. The flatness beside the steep slopes. The echoes of so much life, set against a deep silence. Maybe it was beyond tangible description. I felt a collection of words drift through my head before I could catch them.

Hush. Here is where the land meets the sky. Here is where the bowels of the earth once exploded into the sun. Here is where black blood came to cover the red land.

Everything had ended here, and you could hardly tell anymore.

We turned the car around and passed again that tall cinder cone, Sunset Crater. Its sides were black ash where trees had, in places, begun to grow once more. The top was completely blown away, left like an open mouth, edged in shades of red. Though red might mean hunger or pain or anger, the mouth did not frighten me: it was too frank to induce fear. We parked the car in a small lot and took the Lava Flow Trail, which looped out from a smaller path that was more like a lookout point. Lava Flow still wasn't a long trail, but it twisted right and left and sloped up and down through the dead lava without giving any indication of ever ending. That singularity, that forceful and specific look and feel, that was what I had come here for today. I wanted to escape into this little trail.

Such a name as Lava Flow Trail implied something exciting, and I certainly found it exciting, in a sublime sort of way. This path was like walking through the charred remains of grasping hands, which were everywhere around the path but nowhere in it. So, by description, it was frightening and safe at the same time. These were the hands that had once reached out of the womb of the volcano onto the surface of the earth, trying to steal the sun and bring it back to the convocation of magma inside. Chunks of rock, black and gritty, made dead piles of rock, some small enough but others fairly tall. The path where we walked was simply black powder, ground tight under the weight of many feet. The blackness had once represented lifelessness, yet trees stood everywhere now among the ashes and lava rocks. Were they life and death together? We who walked here through this charred land, we were not dead—no, not even I.

Everywhere, there was silence.

Not everyone who visited the park wanted to take the time to go down an extra trail, especially if they did not know how long it would take or were trying to hurry to make it to all of the stops in one day. And those seeking a long hike went elsewhere than here for the long trails, many of which were hours or even days long. So the black path was ours alone today; our voices and our footsteps felt like the only ones on earth. The path's winding, sloping nature meant that the main path was far out of sight, along with the parking lot and any other sign of civilization besides a pale wooden fence on part of the trail and one rusted metal bridge.

At least, the structure had the effect of a bridge. It was actually more of a staircase down and over a rocky slope, but such was its movement from one stable piece of land to another that I thought of it as a bridge. Moving above the lava rocks without always touching them instead of having steps set directly into the slope, the metal bridge looked rickety, like it might fall, though it never swayed or creaked or gave any other indication of collapsing into the lava rock river. Since this rough structure was towards the beginning of the trail, I considered it a gateway into a new land, a place apart from everything else. There was a world all its own, under the shadow of the volcano.

Here there was no time, or maybe here was before the beginning of time's record. Here there was nothing to worry about. Here the greatest discovery was a green seedling coming out of the black ground or a spider web clinging to the red lava rocks that made up the inner part of a broken dome. Where huge dark boulders stood all in a vicious tumble, delicate green lichen grew on their skins. Logs like driftwood sat beside tall, live pine. In the silence of these visions of death and life, I missed Nathan;

he was the life in my memory and I was the death in my lifelessness. But in the silence, I remembered that Jesse was with me, that he had been thoughtful enough to bring me here even after I had tried to hide away at home. I looked into the charred ashes of my life and saw the clean space for new green to spring up and grow. Life and death, always and again touching; life always and forever remaining.

The only problem was, it had been a very long time since these volcanoes had erupted, a long time before the land had begun to heal. I did not have so many years to wait. And, beauty of the green aside, lava and ash alone were breathtaking. The green made you smile, but the dried lava absolutely took your breath away. That kind of effect, well, it was hard to resist.

XIII.I

I could go without sleep today, I had told myself. I had work to catch up on, and if I wanted to be diligent with my tasks, then I could do such a little thing as giving up one night. One waking night would mean little in comparison to hundreds of restful nights throughout the year. And maybe I would be successful at staying awake the whole time without too much struggle. As the hours went on, however, I learned that my quest for success was the difficulty: every moment of consciousness became complicated. Consciousness became a struggle all of its own, apart from anything else that was happening. It was therefore difficult to focus on my work, the very thing for which I was giving up on sleep. The piles of papers looked too thick and the words on them were confusing. I kept rereading as I tried to stay awake, and that made my progress slow. I had enough consciousness to be mad at myself for moving slowly, but this was not enough to stop the struggle that was going on.

With each blink that I took, it was as if my eyes were taking in a delicious aroma; the feeling was so sweet. Having my eyelids cover my sore eyes was wonderful: the lids became warm arms comforting a child. My eyes were the child, and the lids' embrace was stable and strong like safety and protection, endlessly drawing me in. But since I was persistent in lifting up my lids again each time rather than letting them stay down, the beautiful feeling was not unaccompanied: it was bruised by the pain of my open, exposed eyes that came without fail every time. What was even worse than this pain was knowing that I was consciously choosing to open my eyes to it after each lovely blink.

The two sensations, comfort and pain, confused me until I did not know what to think of my eyelids or the eyes within. Blinking itself turned into confusion: maybe if I was trying so hard to keep my eyes open, that was the more comfortable option, not shutting my eyes. I almost believed this possibility, the opposite of truth though it was, and I kept on closing and opening my eyes without remembering what any of it meant.

Then it became the sleepiness in my head, not my eyes, that tried to prevent me from remaining awake. This seemed a simple barrier. If I could remain in control of my head, then I could keep myself awake. And I thought I could do that much.

Control, though, was a slippery thing. I had underestimated it: I had imagined that even as my blinks grew more vicious and my yawns more threatening, I would retain control still over my mind. Odd it was, then, that my mind was what failed in the end, even when I could still fight the body that held it. The hours passing had proved wrong my notions of control. The top of my head, right in the very middle, grew more and more numb with each blink; the numbness, intangible and strong, was nothing with which I could fight. Working at my eyelids every day to keep them moving was something normal and usual, so working at them a little harder for one night wasn't too much to ask. But when the mind slowed, there was nothing, no way to help it. Nothing could stop numbness: it changed the very shape of Thought, which was the basis of control. Turned half into liquid, the mind emptied into a form of vulnerable velvet, ready to fall down into the nearest chance of sleep.

I supposed it was a natural defense. Everything needed direction, something to control it. When a ship's captain could no longer steer safely, he brought the ship to harbor so that he could rest without letting her sink in the absence of his control. Whether a ship or a body, it was all the same. The mind needed to have control, or anything could happen. So before the approach of dawn came into the sky and before the hours of the night were completely spent, my eyelids closed at last and my ship fell asleep as soon as my mind drifted away into a blurry cloud.

I hadn't met either of my goals: I hadn't succeeding in staying awake and I hadn't caught up with my work yet. I had failed in my assumption about my own mind and realized that I barely knew anymore what it was or wasn't capable of. The only positive to come out of this realization was my pondering about my incorrect prediction that I would be able to fight against my eyelids while I stayed in control of my mind. I had predicted this situation opposite to how it had turned out—so if I had been so wrong about what I couldn't do, then perhaps I had also limited what I could do.

XIII.II

Abigail closed her eyes. Then she fought them back open in a flurry. Neither action felt any better. If the comfort of sleep did not come, there was no pleasure in closed eyes. And if the goodness in life was gone, open eyes meant nothing: there was nothing to see. Abigail did not understand anything anymore; she had grown tired. Days came in which she felt better or worse, but they made no difference to her continuing mourning, which was now showing itself to be greater than single days or moments. Tonight, she stayed beneath her blanket in the warm night and wondered how to think, what to focus on. Only the sad moments were coming to her right now. She thought back to the day that Grey had not returned with the others, to the day when the hope she had held onto faded away to a secret place where she could no longer find it. That was the day when her resolution had fallen into confusion.

Everyone here told her it had been the same type of situation for them when she had first come to the camp. Abigail had never thought of this before. They had expected to see a man and a woman approaching, and it was a man and a woman who had approached. But the woman had not been right; she had not been Alice, though it was Alice they had expected to come with Grey. Yet they had still greeted Abigail openly, not letting her see all of their sorrow at Alice's loss. They had known better than to let that sorrow multiply, and consequently Abigail had found, what was it, only sunlight in their welcome.

As much as that welcome had meant to her, she could not, however, do the same for the man who came in Grey's place, for he was, unintentionally, replacing him. If Grey was gone now, too, then Abigail could greet no one new and could not hide her grief for the sake of a stranger. She didn't even want to see him, if she could help it; in any case, he didn't know her and wouldn't miss her presence, if he even noticed her absence. So she drifted away more often now from the main group, accompanied by no one besides Sylvia and often by no one at all. Maybe none of theses people would be alive tomorrow, either. That was just the reality. She didn't want to stay to watch them die away or wait until they cared enough about her that her death also would become such a loss.

Lives were fleeting across the desert and dissipating like stardust across the atmosphere, and Abigail was troubled by this reality. A great blaze came and looked as if it would never leave; then, all at once, nothing remained. The cycle did not appear to be anywhere near the end. And so the whole world must have been at a loss for everyone who was and would be gone, without recovery. Remembrance still existed. That helped. But if a person could live on in memory, what would happen when there was no one left to remember him anymore? Grey had remembered Alice, but he was now gone and his memories of her with him; Abigail remembered Grey, but she could not do so forever. His memory also would fade when Abigail's days ended. None of them would live forever, and the ties that bound them would change eternally.

Abigail looked to the skies. Her eyes made an endless journey through everything seen and unseen, picturing everything that was beyond their small scope. She retraced the tracks of the stars and matched again the curves of the constellations to the paths of the cactus roots down below. She saw the glitter of the stars reflected in the sleeping flowers. Everywhere, she tried to match both sides in visual harmony as if the connection would make some difference to the world. She was searching for eternity. It wasn't here. But maybe there were traces of it, and she had to follow those traces until they led right up to the source.

The endless depth of the sky was an eternity of space. The countless plants growing and the greatness of layers beneath the earth's surface were an eternity of exploration. It was awe and beauty all within a single glance. That much held true. But the glance of every pair of eyes ended in death, caused by this very same earth of beauty; death must always crash into eternity and steal away the power of the world's life. Abigail closed her eyes and tried to picture them never opening again. But it was of no use. Living eyes were forced to be awake within the world, forced to see. There was no choice about that: you had to see. What you chose to see, though, was a completely separate matter. Abigail was trying to see eternity.

The night air was calm and thick. So recently, even while the days had brought heat, the nights had still returned to cold; now they were changed to warmth, as well. Perhaps the group had also moved more southward again, toward the deeper desert climate and farther away from the city in the valley. Abigail tightened her fingers on the edges of her blanket, ignoring the waves of heat, and began to count the shapes around her just to keep her mind occupied. There was Sylvia nearby, with her shawl as always; she used it in place of a blanket on all but the coldest nights. Over there was the new man, who had quickly settled into the life of a traveler. And the leader who had taken over for Grey was towards the edge; even if Grey was gone, at least they were under the leadership of another good person. The night watch was just visible, crouching near to the ground. He glanced at Abigail as if noting that she was awake. She quickly looked away from him and tried to make herself more still to give the impression that she had fallen asleep, hoping he would not think of her anymore. Everywhere else, there was stillness as the camp rested through the night.

By now, Abigail knew who they all were, and she would have noticed if any one of them were not there. That sense of familiarity brought with it a degree of comfort. But she still felt new among these people, as if she needed to earn her place among them by means of time. While most of them had been traveling together for years, Abigail had only been with them for months. And before that, she had not been in contact with many people: by Abigail's time, few others in the valley still stood in opposition to Them. She had interacted with Alice occasionally and spoken to Grey possibly once or twice, and that was it. Yet Abigail should have come into the camp together with Alice and Grey, as had been Alice's plan. Then the three of them would have been their own group of support within the greater group. That was how most people came: with family or friends, at least with people they already somewhat knew, even if they only knew each other's faces. But now Abigail, instead of being with Alice and Grey, was alone among friends she had never met before coming here.

XIII.III

The clouds were oppressing me all evening: the potential depression they offered was driving me mad. I didn't really want to be sad anymore, but the clouds would not remove their fingers from my house's hushed rooms and I couldn't be happy with them here. Accustomed to sunlight, I could not accept a long stay with the clouds as a simple matter of fact. Though sunlight made its way through clouds, the passage through mist left it white and grey with no hint of colorful blue and yellow. Clouds were only exciting when accompanied by the purple shades of a lightning storm—and clouds that rained were the only ones I found to serve any purpose. As this day was, the clouds remained only a white haze, a blurry dimness that obscured the light. Instead of sunlight coming through my windows on a day like this, only the white paleness, less bright and almost foggy in its gaze, made its way through the glass panes. It was like being encapsulated within the clouds. Encapsulated could be a good thing; it could be comforting and protecting. But right now, it felt heavy and restricting.

I spent some time outside: I was not so shattered as to not know how to escape oppression. I made a change for the better. But this was only a temporary change. The time to come in at the end of the day still came when the daylight turned scarce and narrow, giving me no choice but to go back indoors. And I had grown tired after the long bout of gardening. Upstairs, I collapsed onto my bed with my head at the foot of the bed and my body stretched across it diagonally. My legs I left bent, with the knees pointing upward; this was easier on my back, which was stiff from leaning over the plants. Still, this was not my usual way of arranging myself, not at all, but I found myself folding into this position naturally, spreading beyond my regular half of the bed. That part was more unusual than leaving my knees up.

My eyes looked across to my knees until I lifted up my gaze toward the window above them, on the wall to the left of the bed. From this window spilled a white blue light. It took my attention from the dark of the room, and I saw that, instead of the shadows the clouds made, the quiet light could take my focus. Even as the room grew darker, the light seemed only to grow stronger until the contrast convinced me that the clouds were not the same as the dark and I was only wasting my energy by trying to fight them. More and more, the blue light became imbued with a rich silver hue; perhaps the riches helped it to prep a shade of royal blue for the night sky, a sky undimmed by the clouds that had settled across the afternoon and evening.

A light switched on behind me; it was a lamp I kept on a timer. I had set it up so that I wouldn't have to walk into a room both lonely and dark anymore. Sometimes it had made me feel better, somewhat, to cast away some of the shadows, but tonight I was not overly fond of the lamplight. Its artificial glow was trying to prove itself to the light of the dusk that had held me so enthralled. What with the distance of the artificial light several feet away and the paleness of the natural one, the two lights were of essentially equal strength to me from where I watched them.

So I judged them together. One was much more beautiful, yet also more difficult to grasp: it could change without warning and I could never hold it in my hand. The indoor light, yellowed though it was, stayed steadily pouring from the lamp while the window's glow richened and faded. But maybe closeness did nothing to make the lamplight more preferable: I went on staring at the growing twilight instead, wishing that the blue were water that I could drink. I felt such a thirst for a water of clear light.

Silence faded from me along with the last of the blueness. Because I had stayed so long unmoving, the sky was black enough now that I could hardly observe it anymore. And even with the lamp, the bedroom, too, was dark. The need to remain here, quiet and still, was gone. So I went out of the room, dragging myself up from the moment. Blood poured stiffly back into my limbs and ran too quickly into my head. My head swayed and my eyes shut, then my feet, which had remained on the ground, brought me back to a straight posture. I moved slowly after that, passing the lit lamp and drifting into the hallway. When I came to the stairs, I wondered where I was going. I had no idea what I wanted to do besides leave my bedroom, or what else I might need to do. What time was it? I glanced up at the hall clock. It was already past dinnertime, a time that had grown much more specific now that I was alone and there were no more scattered schedules to work around. Now I always had dinner, like an obligatory task, at the same time every day, except today, when I had somehow let myself miss it. So I had better go to the kitchen.

Climbing past the second floor, I half paused before going down the rest of the way. It was so much quieter than it had been before and not just from the lack of people. More than footsteps were missing; the artificial sounds were gone, too. I remembered hearing an old jazz tune from the library where Nathan was or YouTube videos from Charlotte's laptop in her room. She had watched parodies with music and movies and dancing. Sometimes she would have me watch them with her, calling me to her room or bringing the laptop over to me. I had been amazed at how well the videos replicated costumes and sets from popular movies, and Charlotte liked to share them with me, so it had become a sort of tradition to watch the new ones together. I wondered what it would be like to watch them by myself and couldn't picture it; they still felt like her videos. And although I'd never been drawn to jazz on my own, over time it had become a familiar sound, a sound I associated with Nathan. There was the music he played through the speakers at home and the live music we had gone to see together. I had gone with three hours sleep one night after driving with him to see a certain singer and then showing up to one of my early classes in the morning. And I hadn't even regretted it because I'd enjoyed myself. It seemed that just when I was getting used to this music, the music of his life, it had stopped.

Where had all of the familiar sounds gone and why had they left me so quickly, so easily?

My feet fell onto the first floor and stepped through the dining room into the kitchen. There was nothing ready: so eager to get away from the clouds, I had prepared nothing, and there was only so much I could make on short notice. The cabinets were stocked, but the pans were cold and empty. I wanted something warm, not a salad or sandwich. Those were for daytime, not late evening. I poured water for tea. Tea was warm. Then I looked around. It did seem too late to start anything and I didn't feel like making anything, anyway. And then there was the eternal question of how to make portions for just one, or else be left with enough leftovers that you would be tired of them before they were gone. I set aside the question by putting bread in the toaster. I poured my tea water. Then I glided a knife across the butter and lifted it across the toast. Smooth and even drifted the pale yellow butter. With a spoon, I added honey on top; it was rich and hypnotic. I ate at the counter, leaving the knife and spoon in the sink.

Maybe I was just getting old early. The picture of it, so different from how I had lived and who I had been a year ago, now came to me. Children gone from the house, husband passed away, home empty except for tea and roses, job the only social act left. Very little to focus on, spend time on, or look forward to. How did it come to this, and so soon? This was a description for an older woman than me.

Well, maybe that picture didn't describe my life exactly as it was, not completely. No, it was a little different. It wasn't quite that lonely and meaningless image. My life was not so stark as that. So did that make my place better or worse?

No.

It isn't like that.

It isn't about better or worse.

For better or worse? What was that phrase? Oh, that's right. I had once spoken those words and believed in them as a vow. And that isn't the point, whether or not it is better or worse. The point is the now, whatever it is. The point is what you do with it—and what you have done. The choice you make and the choice you live, that is the point. I had chosen my life, and that was what mattered: I had chosen a good one. My choice was one I would never regret or want to forget about. I had chosen Nathan. And I had loved him. And I had loved Andrew and Charlotte. And that time had been a good time, the better before the worse.

And that memory mattered.

So much.

I swirled the teacup in my hand. The water made waves and then fell still again. I sipped the lukewarm tea and went to sit in the living room.

I thought of Nathan sitting next to me. My family sitting here with me and filling the room. But then I thought of new faces. I thought of Jesse with his old military factoids, inviting me out places so I wouldn't stay alone. I saw Sharon with her tall boots and straight, shiny black hair, her hands building iron jewelry out of delicate patterns. I wondered what they were up to tonight. I didn't want to see them—not now—but I remembered that they would come if I called. I remembered through a haze the funeral; I had barely been able to see anything, but they had been there to stand with me.

I set the empty cup down on the table and curled up on the sofa. I hugged my knees and closed my eyes, letting a tear slip out of one corner. I breathed in the scent of the roses I had brought inside earlier for the coffee table; the flowers were soft and tart. Such soft petals roses had. So very soft. Possibly too soft. I felt like my arms, clinging to my legs, were the rose petals, pink and perishable and surrounded by thorns. If that were the case, then did that make my eyes the roots or the leaves?

Maybe that was it. There was my choice. Did I want my eyes to see by strengthening my foundation or just by consuming? The stable or the temporal? Roots or leaves? Earth or air?

I had lived enough in the ephemeral air of grief. Leaves, sitting in the air and doing nothing but consuming, cannot achieve much. I already had sunlight; that was what had kept me alive all through these many months. I didn't need to sit looking for more. I needed water and life now, to dig deeper into the ground to find my stability. I would be the roots.

XIV.I

As I walked one day, I forced myself to look out at the water, but I still couldn't understand it or why other people liked being near it. It looked cold and cold was not inviting. The clinging skin of waves covering the deeps only reminded me of the chill I felt beneath my coat. If the water offered no warmth, which I was aching for, then I didn't know what it had to offer me. But I was tired: desolation cannot be kept up for long. Though I had not been living in a state of entire despair, I had been close enough to it that I was weary of the feeling. I began to think it would be easier to give in to contentment than to live with this aching in my skull. So I tried to take in deeper breaths of air as I looked out to the water, trying to ponder it slowly. I tried not to automatically reject it.

I supposed the water wasn't a wholly unpleasant thing. The sea did have great strength to it, didn't it? And strength is a wondrous thing to look upon: it instantly awakens awe and admiration. Strength, wherever it comes from, is enough of an

accomplishment to create acknowledgement, at the very least.
And was the sea my enemy that I should feel ashamed to admit
its power? The water moved with such force and constancy,
never stopping and never giving up its territory; if it was not
strength, then nothing else was. So I could enjoy this one positive
trait of the cold water.

Besides admitting their strength, I even found myself
pausing to watch the waves stretch towards me. I was no longer
rushing past, and I was no longer frightened away. The entire
image that I saw had reversed, or maybe it was my eyes that had
flipped around. I much preferred the new image. At first, the
waves had seemed like fingers trying to lure me in and destroy
me within the vastness of the water, an expanse so great that it
had no end, no plausible beginning for each new wave. I had
always fled from such an image, not wanting the hurricane to
swallow me. Now, though, the waves were arms reaching out
from a faraway place and embracing the warmth of the land, so
different in its touch from the cool salt water.

The warmth? That surprised me: it was the first time I had acknowledged that there was warmth in this place, this land in which I lived. I didn't even notice the change until after the words had gone through my mind. But I could see it now, this warmth. Just because it was not the definition of warmth I had always had didn't mean that it wasn't there. Warmth could also be protection, not just heat; I hadn't understood that before. But now I saw it, and I suddenly knew that land always offers some kind of warmth: whether it is part of one kind of climate or another, it always stands stable beneath one's feet. Heat and protection, whatever else they bring, are both comforting. They are both warm. And perhaps the fickleness of heat makes protection the more constant of the two. No wonder it was that the sea would partake of the land's calmness before journeying away across many landless expanses: it appreciated the presence of its neighbor's stability.

Neighbor Earth felt gentle now beside the water, so I leaned down to remove my shoes. It was such a natural thing to do at the beach, yet I had always kept my shoes on. Not wanting to go barefoot or get sand in my shoes, I had tried to avoid the sandy areas in favor of the smooth and worn paths. But that was before. Now I wanted something else, to drift into the landscape, to delve into this beach like everyone else did. I had to see what I had missed, if anything. Bare and hesitant at being without their shoes, my toes curled into the rough sand. And it *was* warm, even on this cold day. The surface was cool, but the sand underneath was lit with the earth's inner heat, or maybe with the remains of light absorbed from the sun on a warmer day. How comforting to find this warmth here, on this cold and cloudy beach. It was like a part of Home had come here to be with me, and I had only just realized its presence. Had it been here all along, just waiting for me to see it?

XIV.II

It was black, the desolate earth in her eyes. Mud and moss decaying in a mess of gnarly roots at the very depths of the world created a haze of death in everything Abigail beheld. Whatever light and warmth she might have found were gone once more in this new time of the year that gave no welcome to homeless travelers.

It was monsoon season.

Contrary to an outsider's opinion, this season was not a blessing to feed water to a dry land: it was a mockery of the healing properties of water. At least, that's what it was for those unfortunate enough to be caught in the season's storms. Every evening, it seemed, the clouds overtook the sky, the air grew moist, and the lightning and thunder came. Sometimes it rained. Oh, but what rain. It rained to make up for all the dry months that the rest of the year had seen. The drops that escaped the clouds were like an overturned barrel, sometimes falling straight down and sometimes moving at a nearly horizontal angle through the wind's current. Raindrops that fell at these angles could not be blocked, and when such drops fell against your skin, they felt like handfuls of water thrown against you, instantly drenching your body. The white clay turned into wet cement, hopelessly sticky. The dirt turned to flowing mud. Flash floods could tear down trees and drown the land like a hurricane; they appeared out of nothing and left behind nothing but trampled plants and a river's empty trail.

All blackness, that's what it was to Abigail. Although the rainy season cooled the weather for part of the day, if the rain fell at more than a drizzle they could not travel. Yet they could hardly ever stay in one place for more than a day for fear of being tracked. The only good news was that there would be no enemy scouts out in the wet weather, so they didn't need to fear discovery during the storms themselves. But the storms, nonetheless, were terrible for them. There was all too often no shelter: the safest places would be under watch and they could not risk such traps. The most they could do was to avoid areas that might flood. Rocky cliffs, boulders, large pine bushes, and their blankets were the best resources of protection available. They didn't always help much, and Abigail had never so much missed closed walls and doors. And roofs—she very much missed roofs.

Out here, the storm had no mercy. Mud gathered in between the rocks at their feet and would not be fully dry when morning came. Their shoes were always covered in an extra layer, heavy and slick, that returned as soon as they scraped it off. Every night meant another wet and loud and long storm. Abigail saw nothing but a desolate earth, the equivalent of blackness, when the lightning came to light up the land in bright white. She wanted to escape the image, so she clutched her blanket over her head and closed her eyes before the thunder had a chance to leave its pounding resonance across the land. As white as the lightning was, she could only see it as blackness. Its light did not heal her as the light of the sun did.

Wet and silent, she felt alone and threatened by the earth. Its show of splendor surely only proved its superiority over her— and its willingness to exert that authority. If the earth had this much power, it could not care for her. The earth roared and shouted and screamed away at the forgotten people on its surface. This was not what Abigail had wanted or what she had expected of the land. She had wanted to be part of the simple harmony that she saw in nature on a clear day, but now even the land was terrifying. And she was only a human being, the one race that had rejected the earth over and over again. Maybe now it was too late and the land would never heal of its wounds or accept humankind back again. Maybe they were never meant to live in harmony with each other.

Connect with nature at isolated moments of peace as Abigail might, it grew apparent that the land would always be something separate from Man. They would always be on different paths, and she could never understand the land and all the opposing forces it held within the skin of a single planet. She could not really trust nature: with the beautiful sunshine would also come unstoppable, unpredictable storms of destruction. Fire and flame and flood were all out there within the atmosphere of this earth. But she needed something else to trust.

"Trust to those who surround you; they will not let you down, nor you them."

The words came with the moisture in the air. The wind brought with it rain, coolness, the scent of wet trees, and these words. They were not audible words, spoken words, or words to hear—but they were still words. They were words whose existence Abigail could not deny, though that did not prevent her from arguing back in her head at the soundless words: they seemed to be oversimplifying everything she was struggling through.

"But I have no circle," she said. "These people are not here for me, and I have nothing to give them." The storm did not put her in a positive mood.

No answer came to her mind. Did the silence mean that, in all of her pessimism, she was right? Could all of the acceptance she had thought she'd come across within this group be empty?

The desolate earth, always within her eyes. If only she could tear off the clay that made a haze of death over her vision, then maybe she could see. So Abigail waited in the mud and the rain, waited for the return of the warmth that would melt away the mud. She watched the veins of lightning bleed back and forth, in and out of consciousness. One rooted out across the sky, reaching toward the horizon, and then was gone. One blink later, the entire southern horizon was covered in veins of white light that twisted back and forth. They left and the thunder replaced them. Then the whole process repeated until Abigail wondered if she was missing something in the moments when she closed her eyes out of fear and weariness. Don't blink, she told herself, don't even blink. Stay and watch. But there was nothing else. Still the lightning came and the lightning faded and the thunder replaced it and everything repeated. There was nothing else.

Abigail blinked.

And then something did change. Perhaps. If she tilted her head just so, maybe she could see something more. Abigail saw the rain and the mud and the lightning and the thunder, and she also pictured dawn coming into the clear morning sky. The air would be fresh and fragrant, the sky blue, and the sun bright; the rain and the clouds and the darkness would all be gone. In just the space of a blink, the sky could storm enough to heal the land and renew it for another morning.

"Trust to those who surround you."

Could it truly be so simple?

XIV.III

"Who could that be?"

People didn't often ring the front doorbell. When I was expecting anyone, I would be waiting for them; that meant that I usually heard them outside and went to the door before they had a chance to ring. Today I was expecting no one, so the ringing bell had nearly knocked me off of my quiet chair. I got up quickly and made my way to the front of the house. Someone was ringing for me? Who? Or why?

I tentatively opened the door just a slit to find one of my neighbors on my doorstep; I opened the door wider. She had brought over a decorated wreath for me, though this wasn't the usual season for wreaths anymore now that the holidays were long over. My neighbor's name was Ilana and I couldn't remember the last time I had spoken to her. I felt a little ashamed at that realization: had so much time really gone by since I had thought myself a regular person? Ilana, however, acted as if no time had gone by; I tried to take her gift of normalcy and greet her in the same way.

"How do you like it?" She gestured toward the wreath.

It was pretty. It had flowers of varying quiet colors and a single ribbon, wide and carefully shaped. It complemented the look of my house without drawing too much attention to itself; it had the perfect balance of details and subtlety.

"It's pretty," I said. "You made it yourself?" I knew, of course, that she had. Ilana shopped at craft stores, not decorating stores, and would never buy a readymade wreath. But I couldn't think of what else to say, and it seemed polite, in any case, to bring up her work. She nodded to me in response.

"I was thinking, we have so many wreaths out in winter. Why not in summer, too? They always make a house look happy. A few brushes of color, but not too much going on. Nothing distracting or overdone. Just something to keep the brightness around."

How thoughtful of her.

"How thoughtful. Maybe that's just what my front door needed." Though, once again, the words were intended for politeness, as I spoke them, I also began to feel that perhaps they were true. Maybe one wreath was enough to help lift my mood. "I'll just bring out my wreath hook—do you want to come in? I made some lemonade earlier." Thank goodness I had: I had grown out of habit of being prepared for quick, unplanned hosting. I used to always have drinks and cookies on hand in case anyone came over; it was time I started doing so once again.

She smiled. "I'd love to. But I'll just stay for a few minutes; I don't want to take up all of your time."

I smiled, too, though for a different reason: what else did I have to take up my time? Today was my day off from work, the house was clean, and there was nothing else I had to do. Ilana must simply have been keeping things easy for me, letting me move as slowly as I needed to back into the social world and leaving me room to send her away quickly if I needed to be alone. I appreciated that.

As I ushered Ilana inside, I was glad that I kept the wreath hook in the entryway closet so that I wouldn't have to go searching for it while she was here. I didn't want to seem too flustered or disorganized. Actually, I was very organized these days: after going through every floor of the house, not only was everything was in its place but I also knew where everything was. Quickly the hook was in my hand, and once I had hung it over the door, Ilana handed me the wreath to adjust on the metal hanger. It did look nice, even nicer than the Christmas wreaths I had begrudgingly hung up in the winter had looked: my heart had not been in those. Though I had not picked out this wreath, it suited me well.

"It's perfect," I said. "Thank you."

"You're welcome, neighbor. It had been a long time since I came over; it's my way of a new friendship offering." She spoke as if it were her fault and not mine that it had been so long. But maybe it didn't matter whose fault it was: no one was really to blame for the aftermath of what had happened. I had needed my time alone, and if she had visited before I probably wouldn't have welcomed her; I was certain she knew that, too. Now I needed to not let her down with her promises for a new start.

"Accepted. Let's go find that lemonade."

We sat at the kitchen table, and I tried to remember why I hadn't spoken with Ilana in so long. She was good company and she was home more often than not, hence the hobbies like wreath-making. She and her husband were both retired; they had one son who lived out of state. She was so nearby that if I ever needed anything, or someone, then it was a shame not to think of her; I hoped I could also be as available to her in the future. Somehow, before, I had never gotten to know her and her husband on more than friendly neighbor terms, though that had been enough for the time: we had still enjoyed one another's company at get-togethers and holiday parties. It was, after all, a pleasant street of people and I had never isolated myself within my own home—until now.

But I had never been simply "I" while living in this house; it had always been "we." Charlotte had sometimes gone to visit a friend on this street who was around her age; I would go to pick her up and chat with the girl's mother, Anne. I'd asked Anne to drive Charlotte to school a couple of times when Nathan and I both couldn't, or I'd let her daughter stay over a night when she and her husband were out of town. From time to time, Nathan and I would go out to dinner with neighbors, other couples. Or the three of us would go together to family gatherings, for Christmas or the Fourth of July; sometimes we would just happen to see neighbors at the Square during an event and pause to say hello and then end up sitting next to each other. And so it was for most of the people here, who were either families or couples. The only exception I could think of was the widower who kept the blue house on the corner. Most of the houses on the first part of the street were too big for just one person, and people who became single while living in them did not stay long. Was that what I should do now that enough time had passed since it had happened that I wouldn't just be fleeing? Should I leave?

But where would I go? I had no reason to leave Prescott since this was where I worked, and I loved nowhere in Prescott more than here. I wouldn't want to move to a newer neighborhood of tract homes, or an out of the way street somewhere. I had planned so long to live in a historic house right in the middle of town like this to leave it after less than ten years. As I looked across the table at Ilana, I found that I did not want to leave my neighbors, either. Though my place in this community would be different now, still I did not want to give it up. Maybe this moment right now was proof that I didn't have to. As the two of us sat at the table, she told me more about how she had made the wreath and gave me an update on her son, who had recently finished medical school. Ilana spoke of the distance between them and their last trip to go visit him. The plane ride had been long but the trip otherwise good, she said. I listened to her stories, and she knew not to feed me questions I didn't want to answer.

Ilana stayed for half an hour, until our glasses were empty, her stories had come to an end, and I had begun to feel vaguely social again. I sent her home with a bouquet of fresh roses from my garden and a promise to talk more soon—and I meant it. After she left, the house did not feel so empty. Her presence brought life and memory back in and not just for the moment. I decided that if I filled this house with friends and company once more, then maybe it wouldn't be too big for just me to live in.

I went back to my quiet chair, bringing with me this time a pair of photo albums. I flipped fairly quickly through the wedding and baby pictures, though they were usually the most treasured of all. Today, however, I wanted to linger on the vacation images: somehow those seemed the most carefree. They were the impromptu moments of happiness, memories built on the most random of events. A seagull stealing the flag off of our sandcastle or Charlotte and I laughing while chasing her sandal down a river in New Mexico. I slipped off my shoes and put my feet on the chair so that I could sit with the album a while longer.

The rest of the evening faded with a gentle passage of time, and I felt calm. I didn't feel healed, but I felt alive. I had looked back with fondness and not pain at those collected images. And I had remembered that there were other people in the world besides me and my loss, and that was progress. Maybe it wasn't progress enough for forever, but it was progress enough for now.

As nighttime came, I moved from my quiet chair to my quiet bedroom, and still the world was calm. Calm, tense air gathered around me and held me up just enough to lull me to sleep without any worry. There was silence only for now, in this moment, but it was enough. With this moment, I would be able to rest my mind and to prepare for the next stage.

Where the land met the sea, many more opposing objects came together. The water met dry earth, and deep blue met pale tan. Soft sand met jagged rocks. Even warmth met cold. To me, it was all meaningless contrast, and both sides would have been better off keeping to themselves. They didn't even blend into one after sitting so closely, like blue paint mixed with red to create purple. And if they didn't blend, then I took it to mean that they wanted to stay themselves without any outer influence, so there was nothing for them to gain by coming together. A landscape ought to make more sense than this. It ought to make up its mind about what it was. Soft or harsh, hot or cold, I just wished it would choose a side already and stop this endless contrast.

I looked on the threshold to the beach. A flower was sitting there, growing out of the uncertain landscape. What was it doing there of all places? I didn't know how it would even begin to sprout on this beach without fresh soil and unclouded sunlight and other flowers; here there was nothing for it. There were sand

and rock and weed here, and one flower. Why? The flower was beautiful; the rest was not. These surroundings had no right to a pure seedling, brought here by some mistake of the wind's breeze. I didn't know how a flower would manage to stay growing here in an environment that must be so different from what it needed, so I imagined that it would wilt quickly. I thought about rescuing it; I could take it away with me, take it away from this frightful beach abode and bring it home with me, to the garden or to a flowerpot. I would be doing the flower a favor: it couldn't be happy where it was. Certainly not. It didn't belong here. Determined to do a good deed, I reached out toward the flower with my hand.

But my rescue did not go as I had pictured.

From beneath the innocent looking petals, previously invisible prickly thorns pierced into the cold skin protecting my fingers. Evil flower! How could it hurt me so? I wanted to curse it for its prying ways. What did it think itself, in order to beg for my help like a lost soul, deceiving me into pity only to derive pleasure from my pain? Evil thing. So much for my good deed.

Such a flower had no regard for me or for my desire to help. My intentions had been good, and it had no right to turn on me. In retaliation for the attack, I ripped apart the delicate petals between my fingers, setting my teeth to the tearing caused by the thorns. They grew at the flower's base, so as I smashed the flower, the thorns pressed deeper into my skin. But I rejoiced in my revenge: if it didn't want rescue, then it could have death.

And then I was sad.

Maybe I had exaggerated the meaning of a random plant, imprinting my own ideas of place and comfort on it. The flower, alive just a moment ago, was gone, and it was gone because of me. Where once was beauty now emptiness fell. Just one flower had been there to decorate the rough beach; just one thing had been there that I had appreciated, and I had killed it because I thought it would look prettier elsewhere. Such a shallow motive. And I had been wrong, anyway: it did not need to be elsewhere to remain a flower. Wherever the flower was, it was beautiful, and so wherever it was became more beautiful just by its presence. I had seen that myself, when my eyes passed over the sand and the rocks and focused on the small petals. And the very thorns I had wanted to curse were what had protected the flower from the sand and rocks and weeds of this beach. The only disappointment was that the thorns had not been enough to protect the flower from its last enemy, which it found in me.

Now I felt regret. I wanted to escape from what I had done. I wanted to fade into the sand that I kept trying to reject. I wanted to forget all my objections, built on nothing but fears and misconceptions. Maybe then I wouldn't see opposing objects meeting in a mad and meaningless contrast.

Maybe then I would see harmony. Maybe then.

XV.II

Although, as fugitives, their journey would never end unless the city found peace again, not everything in their travels was terror. The monsoons at last ended. As all times came, all times also went. Sometimes there were seasons of calm, where danger and weariness both rested. There was also beauty, presented in the very land to which they were banished and which could call up such terrible storms. Where the land lifted up toward the sky into miniature hills and mountains, there was comfort; the desert land became a shelter from the world, hiding the travelers in its shadows. Small and short though the mountains were, they evoked power and protection in the way that they stood surrounding the horizon. The mountains limited the view of the prying eyes that sought them and provided a place to lean against, somewhere that almost felt like part of a house. As much as Abigail cared for open space, she had come to also love the feel of mountains beside her.

A valley, where the mountains circled all the way around the skyline, must then be many times more comforting a place than where they now walked, among hills and scarce mountains only. Abigail had known a valley once. In that valley, however, there had been little comfort. She had lived long enough to nearly lose all in that valley, Grey had lost Alice just when they had been on their way out, and countless other acts of injustice had fallen. How could a place with such horror merit being a valley? How could They dare to corrupt a place of safety?

As much as Abigail pondered the mountains and the sky and the trees now, this was a new way of living and thinking for her. She barely even remembered thinking of the natural world while she had lived in that city, though she now looked back on it as a striking location; she had been distracted before by all problems social and political—and ethical. And that was unfair. It was unfair for such a wondrous valley to be turned into a pot of rotted goodness, a place where eyes turned to face everything except the beauty. The land deserved more than to receive glares and to be forgotten and associated only with war. If only the chaos of the city could end, then the land also could find healing and repair its wounds. Then its comfort would return to the center of everyone's minds. Abigail imagined what it would be like to stand, undistracted, in the middle of that valley during a time of peace.

She let the image fill in her mind until she could see every detail. There were the purple hills sloping in front in gentle waves. The blue mountains stood to the right in taller angles; the pine grew thickly on these. The remaining space to the left belonged to the walls of rock that opened up like straight cliffs, still fairly blue in color. In the middle of it all was the rising and falling, brown and white ground, all encrusted with mesquite trees and green prickly pear and cholla. A vein of lush trees ran along the river, creating ever so much more greenery than was normally expected for a land where cactus plants grew. Grass and flowers, crops, and more trees grew by the river. Above, the sky's blue dome kept everything together inside of the circle of mountains. It was like Nature's own house: four walls, floor, and ceiling. Why was it that all Abigail had ever longed for when she was there was a doorway out?

Everything should have made her feel safe. The mountains circled the land all the way around while still allowing for open space within their grasp. Even the sky above was comforting, simultaneously offering freedom and protection. It was an empty and never-ending space that allowed for endless opportunities without suffocating the air, yet it was also a comforting picture of protection standing constantly above the earth. The land, accompanied by nothing but the sky, was more peaceful than anything the rest of the world could offer: it hid none of its motives and always made itself plain. Even the endless mountains did nothing to keep people entrapped, if they wished to leave; the mountains could, with care, be traversed. It was only Man's barriers that came with locks.

Abigail shuddered at the memory of the locks that had once contained her in her old prison cell, which she had only escaped with the help of Grey. That place was ever worse than the endless journey she now embarked on across the landscape, banishment from home though this was. Between captivity in chaos and partial freedom in nature, the partial freedom was worth it. At least like this she had command over her own person; she was free to breathe in fresh air and to look wherever she wanted. Yet still Abigail hoped for greater change: she didn't know what would happen otherwise. Could she really live out the decades of her life like this, endlessly walking and wandering? Wouldn't They catch her before then, even if Their numbers were limited? Or wouldn't the cities destroy the land utterly, until there was nothing to hold onto, if there even were any people left by then?

Abigail didn't want that, not for herself and not for her people. Although she was still young, she knew enough to not want her life's experiences to replicate for others. She could hold on for the rest of her life, whether it was long or short, but what did they have? Abigail didn't want everyone to live a banished life like hers. And what of those who couldn't get out, as she had somehow managed to do? That poor valley she had left behind had turned into nothing safe; she couldn't imagine how anyone who was still left there could survive, much less endure. Even for those who were part of Their plans, Abigail hoped; she didn't want even them to be left in a valley of death.

It had to end someday.

War could not prevail, not in the end. Every cycle of violence before had ended; so must it be with this one. But chaos, however mortal, left blood in its wake, and the blood haunted Abigail. That was why she had not paid attention to the beauty of the valley before: its trees and its rivers and its mountains had been soaked in the blood of pain and sorrow. Too many people had found their deaths there—or had lost the peace of life. The blood would not fade on its own, nor would peace come back easily. But even if the war ended, by what means would the land ever heal?

Abigail did not believe that the violence would endure, but picturing healing was more difficult. Hoping for something to end was easy and natural. Hoping for something's influence to fade away forever was more difficult; it was like hoping into a vast unknown of intangible and untouchable fantasy. Turning this fantasy into reality was like making muddy water run clear with nothing but the hope for clarity.

XV.III

I sat in the coolness of the balcony in the upstairs bedroom; it was early morning, so I had my hands against the warmth of a teacup. From here there was a better view of the neighbors' houses and the trees that lined the street than of anything else. Yet I felt more connected to the natural world here: I still knew, even without being able to see it past the buildings, what the surrounding landscape looked like. There had been a time, years ago, when all I had wanted was to see this land. During that time of longing, the land I loved had become imprinted into my eyes.

That was the time when I had lived closer to the university, specifically my time as a student. Even when things had been going well at the school, I had often felt like the city was spitting me out. Maybe I had belonged at the university, but never in the city. The atmosphere there was all wrong for me, too full and hurried and inorganic. My own place, my Prescott, had always called to me, inviting me to return to it. I had put up with the call when I was studying because I knew I needed to focus on my classes; then when I graduated, there had always been so many other distractions. Work and Nathan had occupied my mind, then family. We had needed to choose a place to live in the city and to raise the children and to continuously move about from task to task, thought to thought. The call had rested but had never faded; I had set it aside during certain seasons because I knew that, one day, I would be able to listen. One day the vision would be more than just a vision and I would take it up out of my mind and make it real.

But during my time as a student, it had been hard. Whenever I closed my swollen eyes, I had seen it all, this landscape. The layered, pine-covered hills comfortingly framed my vision and my life, encapsulating everything within their gaze. They were there, waiting for me, watching me, and standing with me. I had needed them to be with me even from afar, and sometimes it was enough just to know that they existed somewhere. I could picture them and be glad at just the image. But at other times, I couldn't stand the separation from the place that I loved. I wanted to be physically there among the hills, to see them with my own eyes and to feel their gaze like the rays of the sun, protecting me. I wanted to be free to be wherever I wanted to be, and where I wanted to be was with the green and brown hills.

They always were my reality, and reality is dull and painful without the presence of its object to simplify and soothe.

But all of the longing of those days was over: I was back in my homeland of Prescott now. I didn't need to long to be somewhere other than where I was, and I didn't need to fear that I would have to leave, either. Here I planned to stay for good, for better or for worse. There was nothing, not school or jobs or family, to separate me from this land for which I had longed. Everything I had built was built around here, and everything that remained was connected to this single place. I was here to stay.

Was that knowledge peace or terror?

I closed my eyes and it felt just the same as before: the remembered image enclosed my mind's vision. The only difference was that this land was not far away anymore; it was right here beside me. For once, the image in my head was identical to reality. So where did vision fade and life begin? If the vision could bring itself to match reality, then maybe that was the strength of success. But why was it that vision could be both something positive and something negative? Sometimes, the power of the mind to hold onto a longed for image brought hope, and other times the tenacity of the mind to cling onto a lost image brought only extended pain. Some images were to be kept and savored; some needed to be let go. But the mind wanted all of the images, all at once and altogether. And that could not be if there was to be any peace, if the gap between vision and reality was to ever fade.

I looked at my hands on the cup. Then I set the tea down on the balcony's small table and stretched my fingers out in front of me. They looked withered. This was the kind of weathering that only age could cause. Resigned to the idea of changing looks, I removed the ring that always rested on my left hand. I examined my fingers again. No, they did not look the same as they had the first time I had worn that ring: that had been years ago, when nearly everything was different. Age and circumstances, they are both fluid. I looked at the ring; it still looked the same as it had two decades ago. Material objects do not change; that is the source of their beauty and of their shortcomings.

It was a precious ring to me, as I had always intended it to be. After we had decided to get married, Nathan and I had searched for the ring together because I had wanted something unique. I had wanted an old ring, something vintage or antique, not something new from a jewelry store at the mall, something easier to find than a pair of shoes. Nathan had smiled and said he wasn't surprised when I told him my wish; then he had searched devotedly for me. I always found that the search was part of the fun, even for finding a ring, and Nathan had at least pretended to agree with me. If he wished I had wanted a regular ring, something easier to find than a pair of shoes, he had been careful to never let me know.

The ring we finally found that I fell in love with came from the 1930's, making it about sixty years old at the time. It was silver in color. One round diamond was in the center, surrounded by a tight, square frame. Above and below the square were two arches, half circles, that each held a smaller diamond. Two offshoots shaped like eyes came out of the sides of the square and held two more small diamonds. The last four sparkles were in smaller versions of the eyes that were set at angles to connect the four other small diamonds. The top portion of the band held, on each side, a stretched square pattern. It was gaudy and simple all at once, decidedly 1930's yet completely classic. Whatever the time and whatever the place, whatever the circumstances, this ring would always suit. Now was time to test that adaptability.

Resolute, I placed the ring on my right hand.

It looked fine there. After so many years of wearing the same ring on the same finger and loving what it stood there for, I had thought that any change would be unbearable. But the real change had already happened, completely apart from the little piece of jewelry. The ring was only an object, and it obeyed my will. It had held before my hope for an everlasting love here in life, and these past many months, it had let me cling to what I had lost forever for life. So now I was trying something else. Switching fingers would be something in between clinging hopelessly to the lost and completely letting go of what had ended. I could let go of only what I needed to let go of and hold onto what I still had, and I would be fine.

Just try and tell me that I'm not lying, my mind pleaded.

But I wasn't lying. It was all there, and I was beginning to make my way. It was just so hard. Before, when I had been able to picture the mountains inside my mind, the vision had helped me. It had reminded me of a place where I had felt at home, a place I might plan to return to in the future. Now I was trying to create a tangible vision, a new one instead of a remembered one, one that I could react to every day. I had moved my ring so that when I saw my hands in front of me, I would see something different. I would see the present instead of the past. The ring left in its old place stood for prolonged sorrow and the inability to feel anything else; a widow whose best life was already finished would keep her ring on her left hand. That was not what I wanted. I wanted to be someone now, not just in the past.

Now the right hand, not the left, bore the ring, and a woman who would wear her ring in this way was a better image to hold in my vision, a better position to strive for. This woman was stronger. She could adapt to even the tragic, never letting it overcome her. She did not forget the past, but she did not stop for it, either. She held the past as her ornament, a marker of who she had once been and an acknowledgement that her past identity would always help to form who she was now but never would hold back her present self. A strong woman could keep remembrance close to her without collapsing beneath the pressure of so many dear memories turned to ashes of mourning. A strong woman would only be strengthened by remembrance.

I could be such a woman. I had been before, when the weight of breaking had tempted me and I had overcome it. Yes, I could reclaim that identity of strength once more. I hoped, though, that I would not need to become the strong character again after this. Too many times were enough, and I was not sure how far even strength could take me; the image might stretch too far if I had to take it up a third time. To spend a life all in remembrance made it difficult to spend a life in living. Remembrance was only one facet of a life long lived, and if remembrance grew too heavy, then so did life, with nothing else to light up its days. But I could, for now, remember without letting the weight of memory grow to overcome me. I could do it as long as I held the right visions in place in my mind; a simple, peaceful memory was the only way to keep away the layers of sorrow.

Only one vision of life would hold together all the thoughts of longing and memory and tragedy that threatened to drown away the mind from its still living body. Maybe that vision was already mine, but only if I could keep myself never to forsake it.

XVI.I

I began to hope for peace. I imagined it would come to me as I slept. When my eyes were closed, caught up in some dream, a pearly blanket of wisdom would spread across me, and when I woke up, I would have no more pain. I would instantly know what to do and what to think and what to say, and all chaos would fade. Or such was my hope. I hadn't realized it was founded on nothing but a passive desire for change.

As I woke up morning after morning, however, I begin to see that renewal does not happen like this, like magic. Healing is not magic, and maybe I ought to have been glad at the realization. Magic is false: coarse and rough, it allows no space for the individual. That is why it cannot be part of this world. Healing, however, is better: it includes each person, and that is why it never happens the same or at the same speed. Further, as I was now realizing, one cannot heal unless one wants to heal: healing requires both personal will and outside forces. Or perhaps they are inner forces that are still separate from the mind, still beyond its feeble ability for resolution and action. I continued to ponder these things, and found that my hope was growing.

I still hadn't found peace. My days still felt too long, and my sleep was still disturbed. But I was trying things that might help, things like leaving the window open so that I could breathe clearer during the night. The weather was mild enough right now for me to do this. Perhaps the things I tried were little things that had only small influence on my life. But sometimes they did help, and that made it all worth it: wasn't any improvement worth it? In any case, these changes were my words and my action, declaring my discontent with how I had been going and establishing my quest to improve. If I started by making changes, however small, then surely I would learn over time how to make the right changes. If healing was a process, then I had to begin it at some point, even if I didn't know when or where it would end.

I thought of the spilled water again, which had dried so quickly from my wooden floor. That had been months ago. No longer could I say, exactly, that I felt jealous toward the water: I simply wanted to know its secret. My eyes were drawn now toward success; I didn't envy it or flee from it or feel insignificant next to it anymore because now I was trying to discover what its source was. How was the water able to heal so well? How was anything able to heal or to adapt to new circumstances?

Now I thought that, despite my questions, I already knew the answer; I thought I knew what made me unhappy, unable to settle in here. The true question was, why was simply knowing not enough? Why, if I knew how, hadn't I found my place?

If knowing were enough, we would all live perfect lives. We would all, always, know what to do in every circumstance and be able to follow through and do it. We would achieve everything. But that is not how the world is. We are constantly told stories to prepare us for life and many of them are good stories, helpful stories, and yet we are never prepared. Our stories are fairy tales and fables during childhood; they are the stories of symbolism and direct morals, teaching us basic social lessons. In adulthood, we have novels and poetry and autobiographies to choose from; these are more complicated and more varied, with multiple messages and interpretations. But they, too, teach us much, whether directly or indirectly. There is so much truth in stories.

Most of us, because of constant exposure to so many stories, already know so many answers to the questions of the world. But knowing the answers is not enough: you must be able to see and to feel the truth and to decide that you will follow it, and that is a different state of awareness entirely. To believe an answer is to have faith in it, and knowing is not believing. Only the faith will lead to action, so only knowing something is not enough to bring you out of confusion.

Again I beckoned to my old Heart and asked for it to come home to me. If only I had it back, I felt certain that I would feel what I needed to feel and do whatever I might need to do. Or such was how I imagined it happening.

XVI.II

Abigail started to let herself think about Alice again. As she and Grey had fled, Abigail's last image of that fateful valley had been of the tallest mountain point. For a long time, she had not wanted to think about that last image. Smooth and human as were the slopes of the mountain, she had, in that final moment, seen a clear image of Grey's profile where the side of the peak met the sky. There were his nose, his forehead, and his mouth, all outlined against the dark blue. But what was more difficult to see than Grey's profile was Alice's image there beside his; while most people did find a profile in the mountainside, Abigail had never heard anyone speak of a profile in the sky before. Yet she saw the image so clearly in that final glance. While Grey was in the strong earth, Alice was up in the sky, her profile perfectly complementing his. Where the next hilly slope below the peak dipped upward was the outline of her chin as she bent down from the heavens to kiss the earth. The image was painful because of the loss it personified; yet now Abigail began to see the beauty of it. It was the beauty of the land, once again, and also the beauty of two people.

Alice had been a remarkable person, the only one made to so perfectly suit Grey. Though her mouth had held a perpetual smile, it was not the smile of childhood innocence. The joy that surrounded Grey and Alice was a joy aware constantly of sorrow, yet their joy did not need happiness. It did, however, create happiness, some measure of it, at least. They had cheered each other throughout the hard times, even if there was nothing else to be happy about other than the fact that they were together. Alice had received her joy from giving joy to Grey, and he had felt that he could relax around her the way that he couldn't by himself. Grey was always a leader: he held to his responsibility and was always busy planning and preparing and keeping watch and trying to protect everyone. Alice also was strong, so she gave him the chance to share his responsibility before it overcame him. They had worked together, in encouragement and strength. Whatever else she did not know, Abigail knew that much about them.

Both of them were gone now, but Alice had been first to fall. It was strange that Abigail's grief, which had always been so strong for Grey, had been much less for Alice at first. It was only until after Abigail had time to form a relationship of some kind with Grey that she had begun also to grieve for Alice. Abigail had spent little time with either of them, and though she had probably spoken more to Alice than Grey while living in the valley, she had known Grey more when he died than she had known Alice. So she had felt Grey's loss, initially, more than Alice's; though Alice's death was more horrific, Grey's was somehow more personal to Abigail. But every day that Abigail had spent with Grey had taught her more about who Alice was, and now she mourned them both equally. With her mourning now, though, came something more than grief over two deaths.

There was the fear over the past and the future, sometimes so great that Abigail could see nothing else. And then there was the vision of joy, belonging to the past and to the future. In isolated moments, Abigail could remember seeing Alice in the days gone by, walking home at the end of the day or smiling to the shopkeeper when she paid at the counter while Abigail waited in line. Sometimes they had said hello to each other, always in passing but always kindly. Those were the moments, insignificant though they had been at the time, that Abigail wanted to hold onto, though she knew she would also have to face the moments of horror. But maybe rediscovering the joy would help her prepare for the confrontation. If she put away the joy, then the horror would win—and fear did not deserve to endure above joy. If Abigail had only control over this much, then this much she would see to, that fear not defeat joy.

There was something about that image of the land and sky, of Grey and Alice, that made Abigail feel peaceful, if only for a moment; she felt power from that image. It was as if two sides could come together and not clash. The sky could reach out to the earth and receive acceptance, and the earth could look up to the sky. The people could find a way toward unity and represent both the earth and the sky, in full harmony. They were not doomed forever to be exiled from the sky, to walk across either flames or endless miles, either joining Them or escaping into banishment. And when the dear ones left the earth, they were not exhaled from the universe: still there was a place for them, just barely out of sight for those remaining down below. There was sorrow and there was hope. And as strong as sorrow felt, it was limited by what did and could happen; hope had no limits.

Maybe, someday, Abigail would return to the valley. She would stand in the middle of a clear space and gaze upon the two profiles on the horizon and she would find their light reflected all across the land, lifting away all the chaos and drying off all of the blood. If anything had the power to begin the healing she ached for, it was this. Maybe the harmony of two people would affect everyone, as it had affected Abigail. If she had been changed from witnessing a love like that, then maybe all of the world would also be changed. Abigail could never forget the love Alice and Grey had held for each other and the love they had so fearlessly shown Abigail in the short and terrifying moments in which their lives had come together. For the love of Alice, Grey had saved Abigail. Now she was free, free to live and to hope.

Surely love like that did not die or fade away from existence but kept moving onward, from person to person in constant reflections of the love that formed them all. Change would come in pieces and phases, and hope would grow and joy would endure and peace would come once more for its reign. Love would move onward until all the world turned and saw it standing there, visible once and for all.

And what would the world do then?

XVI.III

As if to prove that the city had no hold on me any longer, I did often go into the Phoenix area for one reason or another. Reasons were, after all, very easy to come up with. Prescott was not tiny and it did keep growing every year, but Phoenix was much bigger; in and around Phoenix were more stores, more destinations, and more distractions. There was always somewhere to go, and it was always hard, after making the drive, to not keep finding more places, necessary or not, to visit. For all that I had wanted to stop living in the city, I kept returning fairly regularly: but now I returned by my own choice, as few or as many times as I wanted. Now I used the city without letting it overcome me.

One time I had a row of errands in the glass-ceilinged mall. Though I hadn't arrived very late in the day, time was its own being here. And since I wasn't here every day, I lingered longer than I might have if I were still living nearby. Two or three stops turned into six or seven; errands turned into browsing. I found the pair of shoes I was after in the third store after trying on many others, including different styles that were not at all like what I had set out to find. I decided I needed more shampoo and mascara while I was here, so I went to find those; I may have also glanced through lipstick and nail polish. Setting out to only purchase a new teakettle, I looked also at kitchen products and home decorations I didn't need; even though I didn't buy any of them, they had succeeded in buying my time. I had given it freely, too.

My feet felt carefree treading across the pale floors. I had been to these stores a few, maybe several times, in the last year, but never like this. Today I was in control of what I did. Everything was so simple, and my options were so many. Alone, I could go wherever I liked and for however long, and this time I wanted to browse around. Nothing from the outside mattered. So encompassed by walking here and there, I found myself staying until the end of the day, though I had planned to start home before dark. Yet I didn't even see the skies droop into evening through the glass ceiling above my head until I was already on my way out. I hadn't quite realized so much time had passed, but that was what happened when you weren't paying attention: the world moved. I decided it didn't really matter, anyway, if I got home a little late.

The sky outside was hazy in coming darkness as I walked to my car. More often than not, the glow of the wide city obscured the face of the night in a brownish veil and permitted only a few stars visibly to dance in the dome above. The obscuration of the stars, so beloved to me, was the price for the much-loved beauty of the ripe pink and orange sunsets that everyone talked about. Too often, I had found the price too great: the sunsets only lasted so long and if you didn't have a view of them during that brief time, you had lost your chance. Stars, however, lasted all night and filled the whole sky, ready for whenever you had a moment to see them. So long as they weren't covered by a hazy veil, of course. I had always missed the stars behind the veil when I had lived here. But tonight I looked right up into a single eye. A bright pinch of light, the white globe stared at me and I felt it beckoning. I stood on my low earth and it stood in its dull, brown sky and we gazed on each other. I stared. It winked faintly.

I stood outside of my car, reluctant to go in, and I watched the star. My eyes didn't want to let go of it yet: they were afraid that if once I looked away, they would lose it. I would look for it, but the small light would never again be visible. Hidden away forever from sight, the star's single moment of neglect would be enough to bury it; hurt and offended, it would decide to abandon me, to never beckon again. I couldn't let that happen. I couldn't let the star fade away from reality into a past that was no better than fantasy. Though a single star on a single night in a single place shouldn't have mattered, I couldn't let this star go.

Time did not favor my lingering moment. There was only so long I could stay standing outside of my car in a parking lot without looking suspicious, or at least odd. Leaving be the quiet star, I unlocked my car and went inside. The star was still there, but the view was different from here; it was more like the view through the mall's glass ceiling. If you looked intently, you could see the sky with its clouds and scarce stars. But it would all fade into a hazy background if you did not look directly or if you were moving about without pausing. I saw, as I brought the car from the parking lot to the street and to the freeway, very little except for the road in front of me and the other cars surrounding me. That was a good thing right now: I needed to focus on the road and cars to drive. But practicality aside, something felt missing when the only things in my gaze were metal, asphalt, and cement.

Why hadn't I seen evening fall? I had been inside, yes, but inside of a building with a glass ceiling. A glass ceiling was designed to let in the daylight, so the fading light was completely noticeable through it. I should have seen that the sun was setting and made note of the lessening light right away. And why did the wide windows of the car prevent me from noticing the sky? It was visible through the glass, though the view was limited; the windshield just somehow brought my focus straight to the road and away from everything on the edges. Perhaps glass was not clear, after all. Perhaps its scope was smaller.

Glass was like the eyes. Both were perfectly capable of providing wide vision, yet only the mind that looked through them could decide what it wanted to look upon. The glass and the eyes, they both directed you automatically toward only one view if you did not take control of them. If it were up to them, you would never see a variety; you would never see what was on the edges. The glass and the eyes, as tangible things, only saw one view. Distractions and small perspectives were all well for a time, but sometimes the mind's eye, bright and intangible, needed to break free and see the sky through the glass. That view was more alive.

If the sky and the road were both visible in the windows, then maybe I could break free and focus on them both. I didn't need to keep a narrow scope, even while driving, and I wanted the expanded view. I lifted the edges of my eyes from the road, letting free my peripheral vision. Besides looking toward the sky,

I also watched the landscape emerge; I couldn't see it quite as well as if I were a passenger, but this was enough. I knew this terrain, and my mind could fill in all of the details that I missed just by seeing certain markers. Small hills grew up beside the freeway as I moved out of Scottsdale. Then there were a few paces of untouched desert before the edges of the main city would give way to the suburbs.

As I followed in this direction, the last glow of sunlight inched away on the horizon directly in front of me. Because of this one stretch of road beside the desert area, I was glad I had left late: if you drove here at sunset, the sun blared straight at you and blinded you. It was hard, then, to see the road clearly. The glare was so bright, even with sunglasses. As much as I had complained about the asphalt, I didn't want a blinding from sunlight. I wanted to see other things besides the plain road, yes, but I did need to see where I was going, otherwise the view of the landscape would mean nothing. The road had its usefulness, too, and after all I had said about not caring for the city with its buildings and roads, here I was, taking full advantage of these same buildings and roads.

Now, though, at the end of the day, the road before me felt so long, endless instead of useful. Gone was the carefree attitude of the mall, when time and duty had not mattered. That had been a different type of living in the moment. Then, I had not needed to think or do anything specific; I had been free to forget worries. Only now did the moment mean an eternity of intent focus. It was a basic drive, every curve of which I had memorized years ago, but any driving still needed focus. And I was worried what I would find if I tried to focus on more than one thing at once, if I lessened the monotony of the drive by thinking of other things. My mind might escape out of my control and run toward thoughts I had not wanted to approach.

The mind had frightening depth to its scope. So very shallow one moment, it would awaken to endless depth the next. Even intent focus on small things could free up all of the mind's barriers, all without your permission, and ideas set aside would come flowing back out. Things forgotten would be remembered.

Unwanted emotions would curl up and spring forward. The sky would echo through the obscured glass. Then the mind would pound back and forth, finding chaos in the space between the ideas. Chaos would fall all in a black moment if the mind could not fill in the empty space and make the sky and the road, everything, all bearable to see together. I could feel my chaos gathering within my head, ready to pour through my veins; I watched it from a short distance, wondering how long it would wait. I hoped I could put it off.

I blinked.

What an outpouring of thought that single star had awakened. Yet I had felt so peaceful as I gazed upon it. I should have still been peaceful, or at least have completely forgotten about the encounter with the star. But neither instance was true: I remembered the star vividly only to feel my mind breaking apart. Why was peace awakening chaos within me?

I knew the answer.

Peace was awakening dormant chaos so that peace could win against chaos and finally gain a more permanent place, a place that outlasted a single, fleeting moment of quiet. Peace had a plan, and I was part of it. Peace would not wait for me any longer. And chaos would rise before peace could settle in. That was a frightening realization, though it was a truth that I had already known somewhere within my mind. The knowing had not prepared me; the time of waiting, however, might have helped.

I changed lanes.

I had only focused on the star, so still and quiet in the hazy night sky, because the sky had been hazy, and the star could only come out in the night. Only now was I beginning to see why the night, the time of darkness, made certain things more visible than they were in the daylight. The darkened night is more selective than the day in what it reveals, and so sometimes it reveals things that we cannot see through the distractions, the many things to look at that exist in the daytime. Sometimes it takes a little obscurity to know what is precious to look at.

XVII.I

My soul was rasping through my body, from my ribcage through to my throat, as though I were strangling it with my very struggles. It was there, wanting in all its entirety to be whole, but I had let my body have its way—I had let in fear and worry and sadness and I had let them take over my life's breaths. Fear about living in a new environment had set up worry that I was failing at all of my goals here, and that had made me sad until I had forgotten what joy was like. And my soul didn't know what to do then, so strangled within this atmosphere I had forced it into. It moved up and down through my lungs, forming its pattern with my breaths so that I would notice it. But instead it just grew flat and made my breathing more difficult.

My body was constraining my soul so thoroughly and then still choking on its thin presence because, no matter what I did, the soul was still there. There was no destruction of the soul by sorrow alone. And it was whole; I could see that. It just felt all in shambles because my mind had fallen apart; the mind was less stable than the soul, and when it fell, it smashed the soul, and the soul ached, trying to send the message of its pain. My mind and my body and my soul were all crowding into one small space, and I was trying, in order to simplify things and spare my poor heart, to blur the lines of boundary. But that did not help. I think it made it worse. I made my heart leave by calling it poor, and I only confused my mind with all my ideas until it forgot what was important. The soul was not much better off. All I did was misinterpret things; to say that my soul was dependent on my body was a lie, and to say that my mind controlled my soul was to limit it. I got nothing right.

Maybe they were both lies. My mind was what I used to make choices and choices affected the soul. Was that so very different from the mind controlling the soul? Although, perhaps, it was possible that the mind did not make all of the choices, that sometimes the soul overruled the mind by overwhelming it with certain impulses. But was the soul concerned with small choices or with big choices? And where did the mind end and the body begin? That distinction always confused me: if they were both apart from the soul, then how, if at all, were they different from each other? Everything fell from a tumble out of my head, overwhelming me with questions that did not make sense and details that did not matter. I knew I was seeking answers, but these questions didn't seem to be taking me anywhere. I wondered if I was simply asking the wrong questions and worrying about the wrong ideas. My soul sat quietly away from the raging waters lest it drown.

But then I found myself here.

Standing here on this beach, I looked down at my feet. They were bare in the wet sand: I had slowly learned, in my time living here, that it was better to walk in the sand than apart from the beach where the paths were all rocky. Here it was softer and warmer, and the closeness of the waves was calming and exciting all at once. I had wasted my time walking on the cold rocks, which were only suitable for a melancholy or agitated state of mind, and therefore that was all I had found there. The sand was much better, physically and emotionally.

Pausing for a moment from my walk, I lifted one foot up from the sand and looked to see the sticky impression left in its place, so different from marks left in mud and so much more than the invisible marks left on rock. This footprint was almost alive: it trembled, even and composed in its form for only a time before the sand soaked it up and filled it in again. I turned my head from the single print to see all of the little marks I had made as I walked. They followed an even pattern, though not a straight line. Their effect was definite, though not very deep: the sand was deeper than the marks ever could be. Yet the sticky impressions seemed to make the sand more beautiful for the short time that they marked its surface.

I wondered if I had found my heart, here on this very same beach where I had come again and again with more questions and more anger and more rejection. This very same beach I had tried to hate was welcoming me and bringing me back to myself. My heart was glad; it settled quickly back into my body, though my mind still was frightened by this new discovery.

XVII.II

In those days before everything had quite fallen apart, Alice had stood out as a beautiful person. She had greeted Abigail with warmth when everyone else was turning cold, and even from a distance Abigail had seen Alice's kindness. Alice's hair had been long, a deep brown nearly black; Abigail had always found it beautiful. It flowed straight around Alice's shoulders like a blanket or a shield, prepared to be one or the other for any situation. Inviting and comforting, strong and warning, that was Alice; she could take on both roles whenever the need came. Gray filled the circles around the pupils of her eyes, kindness and sadness blended into one smooth and constant color. The smile that Alice wore was not a mask to try and be something untrue or to pretend that she felt something she did not, but an outpouring of the purity and joy of the heart.

But there was still too much sorrow that Alice daily needed to touch. Walk in. Run against. Trudge through. She knew, she always knew, that that was the only way to make things better; retreating would not achieve anything. Only taking everything in would let her find a way to help. Caught up in such a world, Alice's smile came to represent her complete confidence that, no matter what, they would win. Surely Grey, his love and his help, had been a part of the formation of her perfect confidence. They had both done much for the people of the city in the valley; even now that they were gone, their influence remained and kept on moving.

On that one day, months ago, that Abigail had wanted to forget, Alice had come to Abigail to warn her. Grey had helped to find the information, no doubt. The news was that They were closing in with Their rules and Their searches; time was running out for everyone on the inside. In an apprehensive mood Alice had come, her immaculate confidence missing for the moment. *We have to leave. Grey is waiting to go with us; we will meet him at the old tree.* Words conveyed with terror they were; the uncertainty of Alice's voice mixed up fear in Abigail's spirit more than the words did. She had barely had time to react and no time to leave.

It was already too late: they must have already been either following Alice or watching Abigail. Or maybe the street guards had found something suspicious in Alice as she walked by and had sent word out to their superiors. Whichever way, there had been nothing to do. Abigail had blinked, and then the guns had come in; they were borne by hands, which were borne by arms, which belonged to individuals. It hurt to look at the souls of these people who bore guns to point so readily at others.

Abigail was almost overcome by shock.

It was not the sounds. The scraping of footsteps running adamantly, the leather wounding the wood, did not bring her fear. The shouts that became the burn of magma marring the mountains as they left the throats did not cause Abigail pain. The clicking of weapons, even, was not the source of her terror. It was Alice's face. The horror there was frightening because Abigail never expected to see Alice with such an expression. Anyone could be frightened, but not her; nothing could have the power to move her like this, so deep into darkness. But unlike everyone else, Alice did not stop at fear: when she looked at Abigail, Abigail knew that the other woman would do all she could to save Abigail's life, at whatever cost to her own. She felt the horror not for herself but for Abigail, whom she had set out to save. Alice thrust her body around the room, blocking doors and looking out windows to unearth an escape route before They could make their way in. But escape was not for her.

The roof was the only way out; a quick run across its surface would lead to the back of the building. Jumping off from there might bring them just far enough from where They had come in to allow time for escape. Alice pushed Abigail toward a piece of furniture, helping her climb up to the opening. The door had fallen right at that moment, of course. Of course. *It's okay— you're okay. Keep telling yourself you're okay, and it will be so,* Abigail told herself as she looked at the picture inside her eyelids, the memories ready to haunt her. Alice had given Abigail a final push, setting her free from the fire. But it had struck Alice while Abigail watched from above. The body was shocked as the weapons found a target, then Alice caught herself, managing to manipulate her fall so that her weight pushed the furniture away from the opening as she sank down. Still, it would take no time for Them to throw her aside and move the furniture back, going after Abigail: she had to leave in this one spare moment. But why? To leave an ally, a friend, to save the self was harsh. If it hadn't been too late already to help her, Abigail would have felt that she had been responsible for losing Alice.

The night was dark and cold. There was nothing here that Abigail wanted: she did not yet know the preciousness of freedom. She didn't want to run away into the unknown. She wanted to find protection and leadership again by returning to the warm aura surrounding Alice, but she knew that it was quickly melting away from solid to vapor. Nothing was left in that room now of Alice. She had to go. She had to take Alice's warning and leave. That was what Alice had wanted. She began making her way to the far edge of the roof.

Of course it had not been so simple as that. They had not seen the difference between her and Alice. Alice had come to

Abigail because she and Grey knew that, though They were not quite yet aware of Abigail or at least were not certain of her loyalties, They would soon discover her and she would be next. For now, however, it was Alice they had been after, not Abigail. And when they entered the room They only saw two women. Because one woman was desperately trying to get the other out, of course They would assume that the one who got away was the one they wanted. To them, it made sense that whoever was in the most danger would have been the one to leave first. So They left the one woman for dead and recaptured the escapee, which was easy enough given Abigail's hesitation in making her escape.

Of course Grey was already there when They took Abigail to their prison; They had captured him soon after he last spoke with Alice. He had never even been at the old tree to meet them, as planned, and Alice had never known of his capture. It was primarily because of him that They wanted Alice: They expected her to be his weak point, a tool They could use against him. And it was Abigail They unknowingly returned with instead of Alice. Grey could not tell Them from the beginning that They had the wrong person: he did not want Them to search for Alice anew and perhaps succeed in finding her. Then after Abigail had explained Alice's fate to him, he still could not speak: They would be rid of Abigail as soon as they knew the truth, knew that she would not be useful because she was not the woman Grey loved. So he played along carefully, keeping Abigail alive and shielding her as much as he would have done for Alice. That was simply who he was.

XVII.III

Passing through to the outskirts of the city on my way home, I felt as though my heart were rotting from the inside. If this was the approach of peace, then peace came like layers of flame that chewed away at my very core. I tried to resist it coming: if this pain was reality, then maybe I didn't want it. I knew better than to resist reality, but I didn't want to admit it. I wished that I could separate myself from my body: led by the sight of my physical eyes, my body had to admit the truth, while my mind still wanted to fool itself. So if I separated my mind from my body, then I could ignore reality. Though I didn't want to be overtaken by grief anymore, neither did I want to believe or follow anything that would cause me pain. I had thought that I was alright: I hadn't made any grand wrong decisions to bring me to such a low feeling. But I was here crying out in this situation nonetheless. I felt the fire coming.

As I left Anthem behind, I also left behind the final piece of the city before the long stretch through clean, lightly populated land with few other towns. Even Anthem, just a few years before, had not covered such a wide area as it did now; most of these stores and buildings were new, and I could remember when each section had been built. One last cluster of older homes, which were technically in New River though they was so close by to Anthem, knelt at the base of a pointy mountain. I had always thought of it as a volcano even before learning that it was in fact an extinct volcano, a volcanic plug to be specific. Flagstaff, not the far outskirts of Phoenix, was the area I thought of as volcano territory; still, there was also plenty of volcanic rock in this area. And this mountain was quite the landmark.

It was called Gavilan Peak, a simple fact that had taken me years to learn. I had driven by it many times but had never really stopped in New River and so had never heard its name. Then I recognized it in one of Jesse's history stories, something about a nineteenth century skirmish in the area; that was when the mountain had been given its official name. Though I called the peak a mountain and though it certainly had presence, it was not at all tall enough to be a mountain. The once volcano was a single cone, pointing upward, broken on top as if it really had lost its lid, though its broken look had actually come from the outer rock eroding away above the hardened magma underneath. I could barely see the hill through the darkening evening, but still I tried to find it in the starlight. If not big enough for a mountain, it was big enough for me to catch the black outline against the sky's stars, which had grown clearer as I left the city behind. I pictured flames emerging from the mountain into the night. Orange and yellow and red in a burning scream, an explosion of heat and light from the center of the earth all the way to the surface. What a wondrous sight a volcano would be.

And then the volcano came into my skin. Everything emerged from dormancy and the pressure broke through its barriers. The blood and the magma were one, and my fragile skin was bursting. It was not wondrous, but it was magnificent, the redness escaping out all across me. I shouted inside my head, and I lost all power of containment over my mind. I was so frightened and so very angry.

I didn't do anything wrong! The words fell out of my veins through the tears that oozed from under my eyelids. I would have red scars on my face from this. I tried to stem the flow of water and blood as the silent shout ended—I needed to drive now. I needed to get home. I needed to take care of my physical self first, before I let my burning head take over. Although I could not actually separate it from my body, I would need to put my mind temporarily on hold. I had to make the flowing volcano wait, though the lava would surely burn against my fingers while I held it in place. I couldn't crumple in the car: I wasn't going to cause an emotionally drunken car crash and I definitely didn't want to pull over to cry on the side of the road. But the silence and the slipping moments were so unkind to me; they were sitting like taunting faces, watching me as I sat staunching my torment.

So I stayed where I was, foot pressed against the pedal of the car and hands holding the wheel; I monitored my pressure on each carefully so as not to apply either too much or too little while my thoughts were running so astray. I didn't like to put the car on cruise control, and though letting the speed set itself automatically might be a good idea, I thought it would be a better idea to force myself to pay enough attention to manually maintain it. So as I monitored my driving, I chased strains of thought around in my head; they were errant. Instead of trying to decipher them, I just tried to organize them. I tried to let logic take over for now so that emotion could fall away to the background: I argued out all the little points with myself instead of feeling the meaning of anything. At least some manner of rationalization came into my head.

I told myself that I had listened for too long, too closely, to my heart. Then I told myself that I did not care if I had listened too closely, if I had wasted time. I told myself that all I cared about was that I had loved Nathan. That Nathan had once been here, but was now gone. That this was reality, and the fact that he was gone now didn't matter to the continuation of reality. And then that thought became almost worse than anything else. That Nathan might as well be a figment of my imagination for all the effect he had now, that was horrible. That the loss of his sometime presence did not matter. I did not want to think that.

Now I found myself in a hideous situation. I saw that there was no disguising it, that the events were reality. I saw that his loss only really mattered to me and that it was only an ending if I wanted it to matter more than anything else in the world, if I wanted my relationship to him to be the only thing that had ever or ever would matter. And I saw that I was sitting in a hopeless place that I would have to crawl out of like some miniscule creature creeping from the root of a tree to its highest point.

That was my horror. I knew that I would have to crawl

out of these clutches, and that was what most panicked me. I was

afraid to leave behind my time with Nathan, with my family, and

to let them slip away into my past like half-remembered

childhood. I knew that the perfection of a child's innocence is

marred when it is recalled through adult eyes; the adult eyes can

never remember, not fully, what it felt like to be an innocent. And

in that way would I forget all that had once been dear and change

everything that had once been real. Memory is always

manipulated by the present, and the historian always projects the

contemporary onto the historical. There is no way to avoid this

corruption, and there is usually no need to try; the manipulation

creates its own interest and value when it comes to history, but

the changing of personal memory is more painful. I would create

new meanings and contexts for my remaining memories, and

nothing would be the same as it had once been. The purity of

experience would be gone. I would remember Nathan and

Andrew and Charlotte, but not in the same way. Time would

make certain details fade and would enhance others

unrealistically. There would be little to separate my memory from my imagination.

My car sped to the left of a deep canyon, and everywhere stretched a blank sky of stars lifted over everlasting expanses of land. Open and endless, the atmosphere breathed out clarity that I was afraid would choke me. I couldn't tell if the mountains to my left, opposite the canyon, were barriers or guardians. They were tall, and height could mean safety, but it could also be foreboding in its powerfulness. If I didn't match the standards of these mountains, then they would toss me out of their domain. Everything here felt wide and glowing, and my chaotic thoughts seemed like intruders on the peaceful night. Just as chaos did not belong in the car, it did not belong in this starlit land, either.

I tried to hold myself together in thought, keeping my bones aligned and my skin in place. My efforts would work, so long as my blood did not decide to burst out of my veins once again; I had no control over the blood once it began pouring out. So I held tightly, keeping myself as still as I could while driving the car. Maybe if I held still, I would take up less space and be less of a chaotic presence on this peaceful and alluring world. To hold still might let me imitate the quiet stillness of this land of mountain, canyon, and prairie, and though imitation in itself was false, imitation could sometimes lead to real adoption of new traits.

The stars shined down on me and their bright twinkle, clear and eternal against the deep blue, reminded me of all that I had lost.

And I decided that I could not part with them or with him. I wanted him to live on in the right place in my mind, present but not overcoming, for as long as I would live, and if the pain was the only way that I could remember him here with me and even if my memories would change with time, then I would bear the pain. Memory, such as it was, I would not forsake. From pain I would not flee, though it might be all too much to bear. I would withdraw into myself, living through my sorrow, until I could accept that I had lost him and find the sorrow beneath my feet. That was the only way. The clouds never denied the rain, the moon never denied the sun's light, and the ocean never denied the waves. What was once begun must finish. What had been started must be seen through to the end. I had to let this grief end, even if I had never chosen to have it begin. I decided my only course. I would let this emotion take me over. I would succumb to it. I would embrace the sorrow so fully that surely one of us would be strangled.

I almost smiled now as I finally took the exit off the highway toward Prescott. In a way, I was looking forward to the collapse. I imagined what it would be like to stop worrying about overcoming sorrow's grasp and delighted in how it would feel to give in to the long denied feelings. But I didn't realize where giving in and abandoning worry would take me. Beneath the layer of raw feelings, I would find something more, some reminder of forgotten stability I had been pushing away while I drowned by myself in tears.

XVIII.I

These days, I pondered strangely. It was this tree. My limbs ached from clinging to it, but I could not resist putting them through further torment: with each step that my mind took up amongst the incongruous branches, my limbs thrilled. As my arms and legs stretched under my fey will, they smiled in excitement. So my heart, too, sped onwards. My thoughts held onto the tree and my hands reached out to touch it. As I felt the contours of the branches, with their varying textures of smooth and rough bark, and made myself familiar with the way that the tree grew, I began to entertain a new strain of consciousness. My entire way of thinking was changing, because everything that I saw was beginning to look different.

This tree was good. Whatever else I could not see, this was becoming obvious. The black tree was not dark and foreboding, as I had once found it, but clear and comforting and alive. I must have been visiting it every day not just to understand it, but also simply because it made me feel better. If I was living

they left space for one another while at camp, during traveling there was no need for so much distance. Closeness was better. It was better for guarding against discovery and it was better for ease of walking. The unity of the people did not end when it met the earth, either: they did not want to reject the land, nor let it reject them. The brown and green of their clothing mixed with the dirt and the small trees through which they walked. Here was the desert's color palette. In a cornucopia of earthy shades, all was colorful, yet nothing was harsh. Warm brown, rich green, golden yellow, mellow red, dusty purple. All was strong and warm and steady. It was more eternal this way. The sky remained the brightest color, a brilliant blue lit up so deeply by the sun that it pulsed out its colorful light all across the mellow land until even the lightest shades of yellow gravel appeared bright as fragments of gold.

When the group passed through sections that were rocky or steep, pairs formed to help each other with the climb. No one was left behind in this way, and no time was wasted: individual toil was much harder than unified toil. And there was no triumph in saying that anyone was not worth the extra effort; that was what They would say and it was not true. Abigail, when the pairs formed and the division came, found herself among the strong, possibly for the first time in her life. Walking alongside her friend Sylvia, it was Abigail who helped the older woman this time, though with a different sort of aid than Sylvia had given to Abigail for her tired mind and heavy heart. No change had felt better than for Abigail to suddenly find herself on the side of the strong: it meant she had not been defeated. It meant that, whatever weakness she may have had in other things or at other moments, Abigail was not weak. She, too, had strength to give, and it was the strength of endurance and resolution that she and Sylvia had in common, though the placement of their individual strengths differed.

At the fading of the sun, they ended their toil and their camp became the light of home, with or without physical light and permanency. Even if they were here only for a night, this gathering could be a place of comfort. If their home was within, then they could also project it outward to wherever they happened to be, and everything that they respected and were grateful for in the land would always be around them. The group slept together on the darkened surface of the earth, and it felt as though the sky existed just for them, to stand above them and encompass their entire scope of sight within its protection and love. For something so commonplace, the night sky had a remarkable sense of safety, and perhaps its commonplaceness was part of the reason for its comfort. As Abigail looked up at it from the earth below, she always found the deep blue sky so full of texture and softness. Yet within it, the stars were still, past all ability to be coaxed or pushed out of place; they were formed of adamant, choosing light over darkness.

So it was here. The world without was in the darkness of war, and it had pushed everyone here out because they had turned away from the dark. But though they were fugitives of the world, they chose not to be fugitives of the light, and if the war was against the light then they opposed it no matter what that opposition meant. Standing united together, however, they were still surviving. And though it was difficult to live merely by surviving, it was better to be outcasts in the light than accepted in the dark. Perhaps one day, one wonderful day, their endurance in the desert would end, if the war ended. Then they would be able to take back their physical home. But until that day, they did not need to walk in shadows, nor forbid their numbers to grow. Abigail had now fully joined their ranks, a new member of this body of people, and she felt peace in the knowledge of the shared company. She felt more powerful being a part of them than of any other society.

All across the earth, their numbers echoed across the land. Though the rocks and dirt would resettle, their footprints did not truly fade, and the land did not bemoan their presence. The earth accepted them, even if the world, which had itself rejected the land, did not. The days passed, and the world waited for harmony; for as long as They denied them and all for which they stood, They had no hope to leave behind the shadow and would continue to keep the light at a far distance. But Abigail had hope, more hope now than she had ever had before. Now that she had lived and lost and lived again, she was beginning to understand what the light of hope really was, and that made her hope stronger. Perhaps her hope might be enough to spread into the shadow, to help lift its haze from the weary faces and to bring their eyes back into the sunlight. Then Abigail's joy would increase once more.

XVIII.III

I walked up to my front door. Here I lived now on my beloved Mt. Vernon, in my treasured green Victorian, beside my desired antique store. Here was everything material that I had wanted. Here I placed my burnt heart, my discouraged soul, my broken body. Here a tomb for myself I could make. Enshroud myself in wooden paneling, heirloom roses, and leather-bound books I could do. Prescott the birthplace of my dreams could, also, be the death of my inner life force and the setting to disguise my still-moving physical frame in the likeness of death. I could let all perseverance, even all hope, die. But I didn't want to be dead, nor did I want to live without hope. And in this desire, I knew that I would be okay. If I wouldn't forsake hope, then I could get through this. I just needed to collapse, utterly and entirely. I just needed this moment, this very dark moment, to unfold myself from all the creases of time's hand.

I put the key in the lock and turned open the door. My shoes I slipped off in the entryway; there they would be out of my way. My feet I directed to take me by slow steps up to the library. If I had to collapse somewhere, then maybe the comforting personalities of books all around would help me. When I lifted my foot from the second step, however, I knew I had a problem: the collapse would not wait. I had made it home, but I would make it no farther. My limbs did not feel the same; there was poison leaking into them, tingling its way through my veins like an anesthetic. It was cold and chill, though it burned with a chaotic tremble against the warmth of my blood. It began in my mouth and hands and the inside of my elbows, and then appeared instantly, disarming me from all control, in my arms and legs and all the rest of my body. My stomach filled with the poison and my head lost all balance. I could barely see or hear anything. I only managed the first section of steps before I felt myself moving down to the floor. I couldn't fight back, and I didn't want to anymore.

My knees were up by my chin and my arms clasped my legs. All on its own, my body had formed a fetal position on the square landing between the flights of steps. I couldn't get out of this position: I couldn't even feel my hands and feet. I put my mind back in my body, resisting all calls toward passivity, and I felt my thoughts screaming as they realized where they were, here in this bed of pain. They begged me to let them out, and I told them no. I forced them deeper into the pain, told them to scream as much as they cared to because now was the time for screams. I did not have to tell them again. My mind took control of my body and made all of its pain physical.

My breath became quick; I could barely breathe in between the gasps. My eyes grew wet. My mouth remembered what it was to sob. I choked, and the night grew darker.

Silence faded, and everything that my mind had let free settled in to overcome me. The fingers of chaos came to implant themselves in my thoughts.

I resisted nothing; I let nothing hide away or sit in darkness. I let it all come into my head: I didn't want to leave anything for later, anything that might come out to slowly nag me over time. The poison leaking through my veins took over gladly and sorrow was all mine until I felt and saw nothing else. Everything good that I had ever had in my life and everything good in the world fell over a backdrop of tragedy. What once was innocent became tainted, and my heart mourned the loss. Yet even as sorrow built upon sorrow, something was changing within the nature of that sorrow. This change took away my small, personal grief and replaced it with something bigger, something even more horrifying to face. I no longer mourned my family's deaths; I mourned now the very existence of death, the sudden ending to the world's life in its every form.

I didn't feel lost anymore.

I felt like I was in a jungle of darkness, where I was traveling a clearly marked path through the brambles and decaying wood. Even if I never once stumbled or hesitated, still I would see all the darkness around me. The everlasting grasp of reaching branches would always be there, however hopeful and right I kept myself, and there was nothing I could do to make them fade away entirely. They would swing in front of me and glare at me and pull my gaze toward all of their faces of death. Here in the jungle, that was where I was. And I wept because I was in this jungle. Don't we all weep? I wept because, even though my feet stood on the path, there was darkness all around. Why do we not all weep at the darkness all the time? How can we not be overcome by its presence? I was frightened here around so much darkness and decay. Yes, so very frightened.

I was frightened not of loss, but of pain. The night grew darker and my eyes were shaded by this moment. I missed everything that had ended and everything that would end. I cringed at the feeling of pain, which would never stop so long as I yet lived. The screen of pain, behind its shadowy curtain, gave me images of Nathan, Andrew, and Charlotte. If I had forgotten them, I would feel no pain; but if I had forgotten them, I would be walking with the darkness that had no reason to hold onto what was good. And I could never choose darkness; otherwise I might as well not be alive. I felt the pain, the inevitable pain of living, because I had not really lost them: they just weren't here with me anymore, and I missed them. It was as simple as that. None of us were lost. I was just trapped within this jungle with all of its brambles. I didn't know what to do here now, here where the darkness, the promoter of pain, was all around. I almost despaired, screaming my pain out into the shadows.

But then I heard words in my head.

The breath is a gift. As the inhales and exhales rustle in your throat and lungs, they connect you, through the air, to the earth, to the sky and the moon and the sun. The breath proves that you are alive as it connects you to the world around you and gives you a life through which to experience it. Do not let down life. The breath proves not just that you are but also that you should be alive. If you were meant to be dead, then you would not breathe.

Don't you see that? So when the sobs rack your body, feel them. Feel them so that you can remember you're alive. And as you remember that, remember what it feels like to breathe smoothly. You are not willing to stop breathing, and the breath is not willing to flee from you. So take it. Let the air guide you back to your way, back into the standing light. The sun reflects everywhere, even into the night.

I listened as the words came to their end, and then I lifted my head and saw that the window was open, just barely. It was just enough to bring in the night air.

I was tired. My mind and my body were silent again now that I could see past the burning and the chaos and the sobs. I sensed something missing from inside of me, as though the poison trickling through my veins had also sanitized all remains of worry and despair. Emptied, I was content to simply lie here and gaze at the opening in the window. The air that poured in was cool. My skin, which had been ablaze all night, also felt cool now. I wasn't sure what time it was, but the coolness of the air suggested that it was deep into the night, well close to the dawning of the morning perhaps. This was the hour of quiet, then. I listened to the air rustling into my throat and waited as the moisture around my eyes dried. Though the loss of tears could have left my eyes shrunken, they always felt larger and more open, more ready to see, after a deep soaking in water. I looked around, and I waited.

I didn't know what to do now.

But the truth, as I soon realized, was that I didn't need to do anything right now besides wait in silence. I had released my pain and my pleas out into the air, and now I had nothing left. Only now, emptied of my worry, could I listen and hear, ready take in what I did need. Only now did I have the space to hear and to fill myself with what was good. But I was just so tired that all I heard was a call to silence; sometimes silence and rest are as important as anything else. So I listened to the call and kept quiet. I pondered the stillness and I found sleep falling into my welcome grasp. Sleep was as much a gift as breath. So I took it.

My legs lifted my feet and my feet lifted my body, and I made my way up the rest of the stairs to the bedroom, where I knew I would find the best and most uninterrupted sleep. Nothing else would do. The rest of the distance after the top of the stairs I passed easily now: my mind was once again at ease, and that made my limbs move smoothly and effortlessly. I slept and I dreamed, and I think maybe I healed, not passively but silently. One final thought formed in my head before my mind slept. I had taken the whole weekend off of work, and tomorrow was Sunday. I knew now where I would go tomorrow. There was only one place that drew me right now, only one place where I needed and wanted to go. It was the one place that would let me finally finish this.

XIX.I

I fell asleep that night in peace. My mind stopped struggling and resisting, keeping itself awake just to find torment in the restless hours. My eyelids were quiet and did not fear to close to sleep, nor to wake again when morning came. I adjusted my blankets and I breathed in and as quickly as that I was asleep. It had never been so easy before.

The sleep settled into my mind and then I was no longer there within my room of worries. I felt myself melting away, as if my mind rather than my body was fainting, falling backward into another space. But this melting had its own feeling of serenity; I was not disappearing into nothing, melting into water. I was still myself; I was just moving into a place where my mind was calm and unquestioning. While I slept, I found that I could forget every difficulty, overcome everything, and let only the good remain, just for the space of a night. Then I would be able, for once, to truly wake up in the morning.

In my dreams, I found myself on my back, arms stretched out at a slight angle away from my body; my palms looked up as I moved through the sky. I was floating through the atmosphere between the earth and the sun; I was free within the space where no living limbs could walk. Nothing visible propelled me through the air, no ship or devices of any kind, yet I drifted forward gently; it felt as though my mind willed me along. I had only to think of moving this way or that way and I did. The pattern of this movement was like swimming backward without the physical exhaustion, with my arms beside me instead of above my head. Contentment flowed through the air like froth drifting above a mug of chocolate, warmth and comfort sinking into me. Sometimes I moved my hands to dance my fingers through the stars, but otherwise I was still.

My eyes felt as comfortable as if they were closed, but they were in fact open, staring in awe at the sights of the heavens, above and all around me. There was light everywhere within this space, and yet somehow none of it blinded me, as I knew it ought to have done. Bright stars, steadfast in their gaze, lit up the swirling atmosphere of limitless color, all set against a black background. Blue, purple, pink, yellow, and green like a thousand pieces of a rainbow arranged all across the view. Everything was more beautiful than what my eyes could take in, and I had no names for most of what I saw, except for the stars, of course. The study of space, as I knew it, was nothing more than the study of constellations, and here the constellations were not visible, only millions of works of art. They were light and mist and pattern, shapes and colors in an endless variety of forms.

I don't think I was breathing. At least, my lungs and my chest made no movement to indicate breath passing through my body. And there couldn't be any air here so high above the surface of the earth. Maybe I didn't need air to be alive in this place, anyway; maybe life came from elsewhere. But my mouth was slightly open, as if it were drinking in the atmosphere like water. My great thirst returned to me here above the world and here my thirst was sated. A draught of light was better than any other, and my heart was glad.

For the first time in so long, I felt warmth and did not shiver. Even space did not feel cold when it was lit up so brightly.

When I rose in the morning, I knew that I would leave the chill behind forever; I would not feel ice anymore while passing by the cold sea and the familiar black tree. I would not draw back and I would not fear, and I would know that the sea and the tree, of all things, were not to fear. The sea was powerful and beautiful and nothing more or less than a body of water; and the black tree was there for me, to help me understand something, about my life and about the world and about people. I would rise in the morning knowing, in full truth, what purpose had brought me here. I was a teacher. I had come here to teach; I respected that calling which I had so casually begun without realizing both its difficulty and its importance. Every day that I learned, I was gaining something more to teach. Career and life, material and immaterial, they did cross over sometimes. Struggle and confusion were all not over and they never would be, but I had overcome the deepest part of them, and now I could move on past that first life I had been in. I had hated nearly everything; in my new life I knew not to waste thoughts on hate and worry. Now I could be who I had wanted to be and who I needed to be. I finally felt right about my life I had chosen and what I was doing— because I finally understood who I was and the world I was in.

XIX.II

Once again, Abigail felt the blood in her veins. If she carried grief within her memory still, at least it no longer dominated her every thought and action. Time did help to heal some things. Now when she walked, a connection to her mind existed within each move she made; she felt not only in control of how she moved, but fully alive within every aspect of herself. Lifting her leg up to take a step, she was intrigued by the live feeling of her limbs, which were feigning being dead in mourning no longer. A single step was not enough to satisfy her delight; Abigail took several, thousands even, stretching them out into long and quick strides. The mind and body connection expanded to include the earth, which was part of the image of her life. As an ant walks forward and is part of the landscape, Abigail felt herself fitting into the horizon.

And as she walked, the horizon changed. The southern lands faded as the travelers moved northward. They had new purpose now and moved in direct routes to their destination. A stretch of green bushes made of pine needles replaced the cactus heavy land; the saguaros were long left behind now. Abigail did not miss them: she knew what was coming next. To the left, smooth and rounded hills ushered in a calm land with short, yellow grasses filling in the space between the green bushes. That was to the west; Abigail's footsteps, however, bore to the east. This path was steeper. Although it seemed, from here, that the land had only gentle angles and medium hills, the hills to the east were not really hills: they were the tips of mountains, though there was no way to tell from this perspective. The descent of the slopes, on the other side, was much greater than their ascent on this side. The level land there was lower down, and from there these hills were tall peaks.

The hills becoming mountains were rich in color and texture. While the pine continued here, prickly pears also grew abundantly once again; that was one shade of green plus another, not counting the various shades of the smaller vegetation. From time to time, glimpses of rock or dirt added colors of orange, gray, and white, sometimes even purple. The texture of everything put together felt more blue and less yellow than many of the areas they had been in farther to the south; here the climate was not quite so hot, and there was more water to feed the land and the people. Abigail had not ascended these mountain hills in a very long time; they beckoned to her and her anticipation grew at their familiar site. Yet she also felt uncertain about what she would see on the other side. Perhaps the view was different now and her sadness would return when her eyes saw the contrast.

But time and worry had not been able to change the beauty. It came on Abigail all in a moment, a moment that increased and grew with each step that brought her closer to the valley. This was where the hills became mountains, where one land transitioned into another. This was where Abigail entered into home. Coming round over the top, the ascent turned into a descent and layers of slope suddenly appeared for her to slowly traverse, step by step; the paths were rough and difficult from the rocks and the steepness and the vegetation. But beyond the descent was open space. Hills, flat land, trees, river, green, blue, white, yellow—it was all there. Framing everything were more mountains. Most of them, including those on which Abigail now stood, were shades of blue that faded into the sky. Towards the left, however, the mountains were red: earthy shades of deep pink warmth engrained themselves into monuments of rock, looking from this distance like a dream of the sunrise. There was eternal sunlight here to protect this valley, so safe within its border of red and blue mountains.

Abigail felt the peace within her heart spread out through her limbs as she walked into the valley once again. The mind and the body, in perfect harmony; harmony and peace, formed into perfection so great that it can touch the atmosphere and feel its beauty. In harmony, everything has a place, and that is beauty. So long a wanderer, Abigail was in awe at the idea of coming home and finding harmony here. The past did not need to be forgotten, yet neither did it need to continue into the present; what once was tainted would be so no longer, and new associations would replace the old ones. If the people were healing, then the land also could heal. This time they would not let down the valley, not take for granted its beauty. If the land could be either a curse or a gift, then this time they would receive it as a gift. This time they would not drown the river in blood and the hills in crying eyes. This time, life here would be protected, refreshing, warm, and colorful. With a variety of resources and land composed like artwork, nothing would stop willing hands. They could start everything anew, the buildings and the fields and the communities.

Behind her, in front of her, and beside her, Abigail's friends walked with her into the valley. It had been two years since Abigail had been here; some of this group had been away for far longer than Abigail had, but for everyone this was a homecoming and a beginning. With the end of war at last, they closed the distance of wilderness to end their long time of wandering and come back to a permanent dwelling. They would

not be the banished ones any longer; they would be the people

who formed the new version of the old city, basing it on

everything that the ruined city had been missing. They traveled

together toward this new task, walking beneath the sun and above

the earth. All around, the land encompassed them in the lightness

of a new day, leaving behind the darkness and the wounds of old.

On this day, Abigail felt safe. She understood her connection to

the people around her; she cared about them and knew that they

cared about her. Seeing how she could help them bring back

healing to the valley, Abigail felt power. She was like Grey now:

she had a purpose and a place within this people, and in that

purpose she knew their community would endure.

XIX.III

I needed to believe there was magic still in the place. I

needed to see it and to feel again what I had felt before, to

transcend my own self and to see the world outside my body and to know that I could be a part of it as seamlessly as the way in which all of nature worked together as one. What had once been so important in my life must still be there within me. Where once I had placed my hopes there was still safety. I just needed a reminder, a connection to that person I had once chosen to be. I believed that coming back to this place would be that reminder. I just wasn't sure if I could do it, if I could finally start living again, and that worry made me entirely anxious on the drive over; I could barely hold still.

As soon as I parked my car at the edge of the lumpy dirt road, I bounded right out of the metal frame; I would not be contained any longer. Swinging my purple bag, a slouchy fabric square with a wide strap, across my shoulder, I set out on the path up toward the mountain. Walking took so long and I seemed to move so slowly that I would never gain any height; I was too impatient for a slow pace right now. So I ignored my slow body and started to run like I hardly ever ran: the way was straighter now than it would be up ahead, so now was my chance to move more quickly through the path and get ahead of myself. And if I had so much wasteful energy circling within me uncontained, it would be best to let it race out of my system now while it could. If I was more tired later on than necessary, I cared little: I could rest later. My mind wanted to run.

Over lumps of clay, horseshoe tracks, and a scattering of dog prints I set my pace. Technically this was a trail, but it was a lesser-traveled trail. It was rare to meet another person here, which also meant that fewer shoes kept the path in order. Rocks and plants made the path uneven, not conducive to running, but that didn't matter to me: I enjoyed seeing the dangers that my feet barely missed as I sped across the land. My run became half a hop sometimes when I bounced quickly from my left foot to the right one or from one side of the path to the other to avoid the obstacles. However it was, I did not slow down. I couldn't. I was not sure whether I ran away from civilization or towards nature, away from the mind or towards my heart. I only knew that my mind needed my body to be active or it would explode, becoming a weightless and bodiless nothing beyond help.

I passed by the remains of a hunter's fire and an ancient, rusty box spring once belonging to a mattress. I could never tell just how old that box spring was; its placement was completely random here so near to the mountains. This wasn't a forgotten junkyard, so I had no idea when or how it had ended up here. I kept running. The frequency of the trees now began to grow and I became slowly surrounded by pine. More often, too, the path went forward at an incline that grew gradually steeper, climbing higher up the mountainside. I knew the views that were available here, of the white cliffs beside me and the cool blue mountains that framed the opposite side of the valley behind me, yet I could look nowhere but at the dirt where I placed my feet. To run here was all I wanted, not to sit idly watching, comparing what I saw now to what I had once seen in this valley all those years ago. If the views did not mean the same thing to me anymore, then I was not sure I wanted to look at them, after all.

But I soon had to stop.

Though my head wanted my limbs to stay running forever, my body had its limits. I had been going faster than a jog, and what with the rough terrain, I could not keep up this speed the whole time. I was not so athletic as that, not after all the idle time I had spent lately, and I probably never could have handled so much running up a mountain before, anyway. I let myself fall slowly out of step with the run, dragging my feet down into a walk. It felt worse to be able to see my surroundings in detail than to simply race through them, even though I knew that was odd of me since I had come here expressly for the purpose of viewing this place again. It was just hard to be here when everything about my life was so different than it had once been. The fact that I had planned coming here, planned to face whatever I found, did not make being here any easier.

I scowled at a heart-shaped cactus pad to the left. Most people would have smiled at it and called it a sweet bit of sentiment; I just thought the dip on top that formed the heart looked like a broken gash, reminding me of my own emptiness. I turned quickly away from a small tree that must have looked completely insignificant to everyone else. But that was where a bough stretched out horizontally, forming a bench; we had once

or twice sat there together to rest and to talk and to look around.
Perhaps we had not come to this trail as often as to others, and
yet still the place was so painful without him that I was ready to
turn back and go mope in the car before driving home to another
tearful night.

But then the sun came out from behind the clouds and I
looked up at it and the night of tears felt over. The sun blinded
me, and I felt like I had just come out of Plato's cave: I hadn't
realized how accustomed my eyes had been to the clouds. I could
not look directly into the sun's face or I would see nothing at all
in the face of such brightness. Instead I tried to look at the sky
that encircled the yellow globe; the deep, deep blue had enough
of the sun in it to fill me. My neck stretched toward the warmth,
and I let it burn my skin because I hated now to think of not
having it near. If the choice were scalding or freezing, I knew I
would choose scalding. Even scalding life, so alive that it burned,
was better than cold grief.

I closed my eyes and let my senses focus on the newness I
felt.

This was the same town in which Nathan and I had been married, when my mind and body had felt so at peace together, and that was why this place remained so special to me. This was the place where I had seen harmony, where I had been harmony. That was twenty years ago. Today, my mind and my body finally felt peaceful again, yet in a different way. Whereas before, when I was younger, I had loved the very images and events I saw before me, picturing in them all that I wanted, now I recognized the inherent nature of the scene. I didn't need to imprint more beauty on a place that was already beautiful, not this time. This time I could see the world without a haze over my eyes, whether a haze of happiness or a haze of sorrow.

I stood on a lonely dirt path. While the mountain did offer wide views of the Verde Valley, none of them were before me at the moment; they were hidden behind the slopes. The scrubby land of prickly pear and pine was simply itself, a land apart from all others, and the sun was as bright as it always was. And I was alone, without another person probably for miles around. Yet I felt the same contented sensation as I had had before, on the day of my wedding, except that this time it was tracing itself from the top down instead of from the ground upward. The heat from the sun echoed and pulsed past my closed eyelids, stretching across my cheekbones to my neck and torso, down my legs and feet to the earth on which I stood. I didn't feel like I was simply standing up straight on the land; I felt like the brightness and openness of the sky was helping to keep my limbs free. Light, pure light, was reaching out to me, and I basked within it.

Maybe I could no longer call what I felt magic, but it was certainly not gone, whatever else I had been forced to part with. I could better understand now this warmth that was not magic, this warmth that was everything good and nothing artificial. At least, now I could see that the scope to my understanding of every event that happened in my life had limits, and I did not need to mind those limits any longer. So long as I understood certain things, the important things, I was alive and warm here in this land beneath the sun. The unchangeable past did not need to hurt forever if memory could still hold joy; even after loss, I remained myself, and I was not a person to stop moving forward.

I kept walking until I reached a high point on the mountain. The path went on beyond this place, but here it already felt high enough. Up ahead were more trees and obscurity; here there was still some openness. I let my gaze free now and looked back down at the valley. It was so full within my view, colored in brown and gold and cream with thick bundles of green, all held safe by blue and gray hills and mountains. The outer world remained intact and constant even when my inner world fell into dust; now that I was ready to return back to solidity, it was here waiting for me. I looked and saw that it was beautiful, and I felt joy.

XX.

If I let my eyelids slip and fall, will I fade into your arms? If I breathe in slowly, will I see you there beside me? Will you be near, even when I am not there with you? The air is stale without you, and my mouth tastes nothing but bitterness. Will I see you again? I want to see you here again—but just knowing you existed, always that was enough. Simply forming a connection, forever that kept me awake to life and to love. If you can't come back down to me, might I come and follow you? One day I will arise and pursue the path you left behind for me. That path is greater even than everything I shared with you and matters even more than my love for you. That is why I cannot grieve for you forever.

One day, pain will go away. And you'll find me there again beside you. And it will be as if we'd always been together. Everything I have spent so many days longing for will be complete once again. Don't say how long I will have to wait. I need to believe in something, and I believe in this future. I believe in all that held me up. That is all I can believe in. That is all I can hold onto. And that is all I need. It is everything that completes me. I see joy again and I rise up in the new morning.

Now I open my eyes.

Acknowledgements

Thank you to the land that inspired this book and to everyone who helped me bring its pages into completion. Thank you to my parents for supporting my path toward publication. Thank you to those who were the first to read this book and for the kind words you gave me in return. Thank you to Cari for the beautiful cover photography.

I also want to thank everyone who ever encouraged my writing, teachers specifically. Teachers have such potential to influence their students, and I am grateful to the teachers who helped to show me my potential.

On an artistic level, I couldn't have made this book without the work that came before me: art, music, and literature. Thanks to all of the painters, musicians, singers, and writers who gave me inspiration and even passed along advice.

And thank you, readers, for letting me share this book with you.

About the Author

Deanna Skaggs has lived in Arizona for most of her life and has fallen under the spell of its starry skies, cactus-covered hills, and constantly changing seasons. She graduated summa cum laude from Barrett, the Honors College at Arizona State University with a degree in English literature. *Black Tree* is her first novel.

You can visit her online at her author website, **deanna-skaggs.com**, or her blog, **deliriousdocumentations.com**. There you'll find more information about her writing and the making of *Black Tree*. To let her know what you thought of the book or to ask a question, send her an email at **deanna.skaggs@gmail.com**; she'd love to hear from you.

www.ingramcontent.com/pod-product-compliance
Lightning Source LLC
Chambersburg PA
CBHW022147010726
47493CB00002B/381